CHRONICLES
—OF THE—
OTHERWORLD

SEASON 1

A. S. ARAMIRU

Author email: ASAramiru@gmail.com
Author web site: https://www.Aramiru.com

Published by Shadywood Lane Publishing in 2016
ISBN-13: 978-0-9862004-4-1

Cover art by Shadywood Lane Publishing

Follow the Author for Updates, News, and to Collect His Loose Marbles

TWITTER
https://twitter.com/ASAramiru

FACEBOOK
https://www.facebook.com/ASAramiru

PATREON
https://www.patreon.com/ASAramiru

"I wish I knew how to quit you."

- Jake Gyllenhaal as Jack Twist in
  BROKEBACK MOUNTAIN

List of Episodes

Episode 0
Anton's Short Story

Episode 1
Tay's Back

Episode 2
Camillla's Letter

Episode 3
Tay's Crate

Episode 4
Bob and Robert

Episode 5
It's Sarne

Episode 0
ANTON'S SHORT STORY

It's not the calm before the storm but the silence after that gets you.

Facing the aftermath of the carnage, the destruction, and the judgment.

Don't be fooled by all the wood and stone that make up the mansion. All still in its place. Undamaged and clean. Nor by the oil lanterns still bright, burning, and hot. The walls tell that real tale. Painted with blood and guts.

Anton thinks he can outrun it.

Outsmart it.

Get off the destined path he set upon since who knows when. He doesn't even know.

He tries to calm himself, but without the screams of his friends, he can finally hear his own heartbeat.

Take a peek, Anton.

Not much else you can do.

Weapons without their masters scattered across the hall.

All of them dead by the same cause.

Blunt trauma to their heads. Crushed like summer melons.

The butchered brains and pools of blood, too hard to tell whose body produced what.

His signature.

The man in the black armor. His face hidden behind the helm with a plume formed by long crimson lights that gently danced behind him like whips. Affectionately named, "Redtails."

Anton snaps back behind his wall wishing

desperately he had learned a spell or two.

I don't deserve this. Anton tells himself. *Fuck this.*

We rarely get what we deserve. But there's comfort in the idea that what happens to us has nothing to do with what we deserve.

Because by that same rule, Anton might even survive.

From his pocket, Anton pulls out the magic from his own world. A pocket revolver. He doesn't remember what the brand is or even what caliber it uses. It wasn't his. He had snatched it from his brother's drawer before he came back to this world.

He swings around with the gunpowder courage and aims the weapon at the approaching storm.

Redtails doesn't stop.

"Fuck you," Anton screams at him. "FUCK YOU!"

A silent soldier on a march. That was his answer to Anton.

Make them count. He says without words.

Bang.

Bang.

Bang.

Bang.

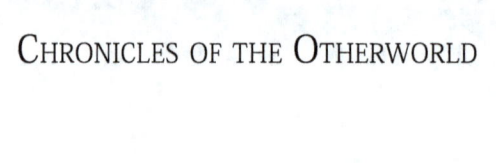

Anton stops for a moment and lets the smoke clear.

Redtails is closer.

Bang.

Only a little further than an arm's length away now.

Bang.

The black knight allows the lips of Anton's gun to kiss his helm.

Click.

The knight gently taps his dark, steel club on Anton's forehead *once…*

"Look." Anton takes off his glove and shows the back of his left hand. There was the red, almond shaped insignia that seemed as if it was tattooed onto his flesh.

…twice.

"I'm from our world," Anton says. "You're one of us, right? You have to be one of us. Come on, man."

It wasn't Anton's fault that he didn't know this was another one of the Redtails' signatures. There wasn't anyone alive who knew about it. A gentle ritual he performed when the circumstances were just right. He had to be in the mood for it.

This is the silence after the storm.

Redtails swings his club.

A clang.

Sounds almost like a home run. As if Barry Bonds himself was on the plate.

It's in tune with the crack of the shattering skull.

Then an almost immediate follow-up performance of the loud splatter on the wall.

Almost a cartoonish noise.

Anton's body drops.

No more Anton.

No more questions of whether or not he deserves it.

Just silence.

Silence without judgment or concern.

Episode 0 ANTON'S SHORT STORY

Episode 1
TAY'S BACK

"The way you ran off last time, I didn't think you'd come back again."

The man behind the desk grins. The gatekeeper. I always thought it was a bit unnerving how he could turn from a complete grimace to that shit-eating grin and then go back to his I-finally-tasted-the-shit grimace.

It's a small office space. One of many in this complex. Except this one, you can only come in after dark.

It hasn't changed at all since last time I was here. The only light in the room is the desk lamp on the little wooden desk the man sits behind. There's the one little flower in the vase on the other end corner of the desk. The carpets were still inexplicably clean. I couldn't imagine the gatekeeper ever leaving his desk. I just imagine him sitting at his desk with his grimace as the cleaning crew did their thing. Staring at them without blinking.

But offices like this feels too familiar. Too stale. It's the exact thing I want to run from.

I wonder what kind of face I have on right now. Probably something between alive and dead. I didn't shower this morning. Still trapped in my suit and overcoat. Why did I bring my briefcase with me?

"Yeah," I answer after the long pause. I just realized this guy has been staring at me the whole time as I was lost in my own thoughts.

The man waves me over. He's not going to ask why I came back. Just like how he didn't ask why I left. He's not going to tell me to think it over. Nor is he going to tell me that I may not come back. That I can die there. Or worse: be trapped.

I set my briefcase on his desk.

He looks a bit annoyed but takes it anyway and sets

it beside him.

"Let's get you stamped then," the man says as he opens his drawer. He seems to shuffle around in there a bit. What else could he have in there?

I do my part and place my hand on the desk. I never did like this part. I could see the mark on the desk from my last voyage. And the marks of other voyagers.

He finds what he's looking for and slides the drawer back in.

I clench my teeth.

Without hesitation or mercy, the man strikes down through my hand with his oddly shaped vermilion dagger.

My legs buckle. It's a thick and wide blade. I let out violent grunt as I hold back some words my mother wouldn't be pleased to hear. I'd forgotten how much it hurts. Maybe my mind blocked it out. I clench my teeth. Hard. Stop myself from screaming.

Don't be a little bitch, I tell myself, beads of sweat gathering on my forehead. *Don't be a pussy.*

I always tell myself not to look up. But I do anyways.

He's grinning at me with a curious tilt. His scrawny hand still gripping firmly on the dagger's hilt. It's as if he's asking me…

"Shouldn't you be used to this by now? Does it still hurt you?"

It's as if he's disappointed. Why do I care if he's disappointed? Why do I care what he thinks of me?

"Pu—"

He doesn't even let me complain and pulls out before I can finish my sentence.

I glare at him. I want to say something. I know he kept the blade in there as long as he could for his own amusement. I know he pulled it out just before I'd say something to not even give me that satisfaction.

Motherfucker.

Son of the dirtiest bitch in the dirtiest corner of the shittiest town.

Shitfucker.

I ought to make him bite the curb and slam down the back of his skull.

I want to tell him off.

I say nothing.

I might have anger issues. But given what's happened lately, I don't blame myself too much.

I look at my hand. Blood still spurting and pooling around my palm and onto his desk. Before the blood can spill down the edges, it sucks into the gap it came from and the wound closes. All that remains is a red seal of sort. Shape of the blade wound. If I tilt my hand sideways, I always thought it looked sort of like an eye. Especially with the circular patch of my skin in the center. That wasn't normal. But I knew why it was there.

"You remember why that's there?" the gatekeeper asks as he puts away the blade. He didn't even have to clean it.

"Yeah," I tell him.

"You remember the rules?" He asks as he gets up and walks over to the door behind him. He places his hand on the knob. Waiting for me to answer before turning it.

"Yes." I walk over.

"You coming back this time?"

I don't have an answer.

He chuckles.

"Welcome back to the Otherworld." He smiles and knocks on the door twice. "You want to go back to the last waypoint?"

I nod. I actually didn't know I had a choice in the matter.

He opens the gate.

There's only darkness on the other side. No light at the end. Just pure, pulsating darkness.

It's alive and I'll enter its womb. It's almost a maddening experience.

I enter it.

The ground below feels solid enough to walk on but not hard.

The air is thick but neither warm nor cold.

I look behind me. The only light I'll see for a while is the desk lamp.

The gatekeeper closes the door without even looking.

I counted the seconds last time.

It'll be about 2,057 seconds until I hit the end. Or about 35 minutes.

I dig into my pocket for my earphones.

I don't need to count the seconds this time.

Episode 2
CAMILLA'S LETTER

"Get this letter to the King's Guard. To Tarron. It details their plans for Coldson."

Loren is still in her formal ballroom garment. Even with the slightest movement, the lace and skirt of the dress dances gently in the air. I find her too pretty to be a knight. Sexism out of the gentle envy and disbelief that anyone could be this perfect. The ideal figure of a woman, the face of a doll, and the skills to end any man or beast. At this moment, despite her distaste for dolling up, her long brunette hair is tied in complex loops and knots to form an ornamental bun as she's bundled in a dress that she could stand confident in even among the highest of audiences. Fooling many royals, teasing many hearts. She's the kind of beauty that makes the socialites and the high class wonder how they've never seen something like her before.

Someday — sooner than later — I'll be like her.

"You mustn't fail. Lives depend on it," she stresses as she hands me the envelope.

"I understand." I make certain my voice carries confidence and weight as I stuff the envelope in my pocket.

She pauses for a moment and studies my face. It makes me nervous. Her emerald eyes are piercing. Was there more to the mission? Did I possibly do something wrong?

"Camilla," she says my name. "With this, I'm sure Tarron will find a way to accept you into the Order. No matter what objections the naysayers may bring up."

The Order. The Order of the Three Talons. The grand military directly in the service of the king formed after the great civil war that almost sundered this kingdom apart. And Tarron, the general in charge of the small section of the Order known as the King's Guard. A unit where only the most elite like Loren can serve. Joining the Order would be my first step in joining those two. Or at least have the chance to.

"…You've done enough for the king and for the kingdom." Loren places her hand on my shoulder. "I know Tarron has great expectations for you."

I shyly smile at the suggestion. I'm embarrassed. Why am I smiling? For all I know, she could just be teasing. A pat for the good puppy.

I watch as Loren walks back into the dead streets of the night to head toward the only sign of life—the manor of the local royalty. Back to the banquet.

"May the great Sarne watch over your tale," she told me before she left.

Sarne. The God of Tales. What tale is he weaving for me, I wonder?

The night wind ruffles my hair. The strands of it tease my eyes. I brush it away and think of Tarron. The Undying General.

The legends of Tarron… they seem like such tall tales that I have hard time believing them. They say that when Tarron was a child, his entire family died in a fire. He tried to rescue them only to end up with severe burns on half of his face and the loss of use of one of his arms. Somehow from that point of his life, he brought himself up to becoming a knight for the King. But then he was only noted for his disfigurements. As the guy who made it despite his shortcomings. It wasn't until the War of the Kings that he became a legend.

The story goes that during one of the skirmishes, Tarron saw a distress signal light up the night sky. A small surveillance group that went out to field the area had been caught in a trap. Even at his age, Tarron wasn't given much of a leadership position due to his disability. Never given the chance to prove himself. But he remained loyal to the crown and served with utter passion and zeal.

Many said that the group was lost. That they were surrounded by an army of enemies.

Tarron understood why the military wouldn't be able to send help, but he couldn't allow himself to simply sit idly by.

When it was all said and done, his bad arm was blown off. Left ear slashed—which he tells me was worth it over losing his better eye. His stomach was sliced open with the insides dangling out. There were a total of forty-two puncture wounds. Sixteen lacerations. And rumor has it even a couple of toes missing to top it all off.

When the day finally broke, the enemies decided it wasn't worth trying to kill this man or the men he was trying to protect. They let them be. Out of the nine he was trying to rescue, four survived. Two-hundred some enemies were reported dead in this incident, but this only came to light after the war ended. No one wanted to admit a single man had caused them so much damage.

The four survivors carried their hero back to base.

They thought he had died. Looked like a bloodied mangled corpse. His men gently set him down and called for the medics and the healers.

The king himself made his presence to see the corpse.

In the presence of the king, the corpse turned to knight once more and took a knee.

They told me it took him nearly a year to recover, and depending on whom I asked, 'nearly' was replaced with 'only.' For many others, they would have told him that he would never walk again, but the medics didn't want to take a chance with him.

After that year, he went back into the war to support the king.

Most people would have told this man to retire. That he had done his duty. He had already transcended from a man to legend. But, for his own sake, the King was wiser than that. Wise enough to be selfish. Selfish enough to ask this man to stay by his side until he passed.

Tarron. Loren.

What great tale Sarne had woven for them.

And why not me? I can be just as great. I just have to prepare myself for the day when Sarne gives me such a chance.

Someday, I, Camilla, will stand equal amongst them. No matter what it takes.

It's late. The air's cold. It's nearly winter, after all. I hear Coldson is warm even during winter even though it's by the mountains. How's that possible, I wonder?

The town's dark. Only the lanterns that hang from tips of the buildings are lit. I kind of enjoy the shroud of darkness when everything is still and silent. There's something tranquil about it and something magical about how all of this nothingness can come to life with daylight.

I hear something.

A squeal.

Violent rustles.

If there were more people out and about, I might have missed it.

But what is it?

My curiosity will be the end of me, Loren always teased.

But this is also what makes me — me.

The sound was brief, but my intuition told me to follow the clues, and I heard more and more sounds in the air.

In the dark alley, near a tavern, I saw him. If pigs walked on two feet, they'd look like him. Disgusting, blubbery-looking man. I can see every curve, twist, and crevice with the dirty tank top-like shirt he's wearing. With a giant balloon-like lump for a belly, he almost seems like he's trying to fit into a caricature of a disgusting lump of a man. He has a woman in his clutches. He's holding the woman's mouth with one hand while holding tightly to her waist with the other. She looks at me with frightened eyes. Eyes that'd carve and stitch itself forever into my conscience if I just walked away.

Have courage, Camilla.

If not courage, then anger and disgust for the heinous acts the creature in front of me is committing.

Besides, what kind of King's Guard would I be if I walked away from this?

"Hey, Pig!"

Yes. Pig is a good name for him.

He looks up. Doesn't seem very interested. Doesn't seem to feel very threatened. He turns around and carries off the maiden. Even from behind, this creature is disgusting. There's a lump, a growth, a tumor, of sort on his back hidden beneath the shirt.

Bastard.

I shouldn't kill him. I'll just use a lighter spell to simply teach him a lesson. Something enough to sober up a drunk.

It always begins with the white flame, I remind myself.

Then we shape it the way we desire. The more complicated the design, the more training it requires and sometimes preparations.

The white flame solidifies, and I form from it a ball pieced together with octagons. It shoots out from my hand and shatters on his fat head.

He turns around.

He seems surprisingly unharmed.

I prepare another one. This time when it pops, it'll feel like the hardest punch he can't even imagine.

"Let the lady go, Pig," I demand.

He listens. The maiden drops to the hard ground and she coughs violently as she massages her throat.

Good.

Then the Pig swings the back of his hand hard enough that the smack echoes as it breaks the maiden's nose. She doesn't even make a noise as her body falls to the ground.

This bastard.

I shoot the second ball at his face. It knocks him back a little bit.

I immediately form another one even stronger than before. I pour ether into it until it becomes a solid sphere. It hums. This one will feel like a giant, furious horse kicking him in the face. Before he can even tilt his head back from the last blow, the third orb hits him and it lifts him off his feet.

He's down.

I run after the girl. Her face is red. It's swollen, and

it'll be bruised by tomorrow. Her nose is broken, but I'm not sure how to set it. A lot of blood. She's barely older than I am. Her attire, seems like she's been traveling. Probably got taken advantage of as she was exploring the town.

I can't carry her.

I don't think I know any spells that can help me drag her out of here.

"Hey, hey," I try to wake her by gently shaking her.

I look up.

The Pig is glaring at me. Blood is gently streaming down his nose.

When did he get up?

"You better get going," I tell him. "Sleep it off."

I conjure up another orb. Just as strong as the last one.

I flick my finger, and the orb is now gently hovering by my head. If the Pig tries anything, it'll fire at him. I tend to the unconscious traveler.

The orb fires at the Pig. I hear the last shatter and the impact.

But immediately after, I inexplicably feel his giant, chubby hands smacking across the side my head.

For a moment, everything turns black.

My ear rings like knife against glass.

Then, another smack on the other side, and I'm on the ground.

He grabs my ankle with a grip that feels like he's going to tear the skin off the muscle. He pulls me further into the darkness of the alley. Away from the traveler.

I have to get it together.

"The fire within us all…"

Before I can finish my incantation, the Pig swings me around and my entire body smacks against one of the walls of the buildings.

Everything turns black again.

I feel like throwing up.

How am I alive?

Why didn't that wake anyone up?

I don't even realize when he flips me over and puts me in a choke hold. Everything is a blur. Painful blur.

I can't breathe.

I feel like my neck is being crushed into dust.

My head feels hot. It's going to explode.

I'm going to die.

My mouth gapes open trying desperately to suck in air, but all it does is dry out my mouth.

I'm going to die.

No. I can't give up.

I flail my arms and legs. I try to conjure up more spells, but I can't concentrate.

Is it fear? Is it the pain?

I'm not worthy of being part of the Order.

I look at the damsel I was trying to save.

She's awake and looks horrified. Her eyes are watering up, but she's standing. Her face is a bloody mess.

I reach out to her.

She shakes her head and mouths me something.

And then she takes off.

I start to add everything up as my consciousness begins to wane.

That woman wasn't a plain traveler. Her attire, all the pieces, now I can add it all up. The necklace around her neck isn't just a necklace. It's an amulet. I can make out inside of her cloak seamed with sigils. Small pouches around her waist probably are filled with ingredients for sorcery. She's a wizard. An adventurer. Probably an experienced one. Probably better than me.

She wasn't frightened for her life.

She was frightened for mine.

She wanted me to walk away. Let her be taken.

She knew that she would be helpless to help if I was caught.

She knew both of us would die to this Pig.

Should a person try to save a drowning child if she didn't know how to swim?

Maybe I would.

Mom.

***

Sore.

I'm alive?

Entire body aches.

It's freezing.

And it reeks.

Reeks of… mold… wet stone… and old meat. Rancid. Wretched.

Something's dripping somewhere.

I'm pretty sure my eyes are open, but I can't see anything. I hope it's just dark.

I feel like throwing up. My insides all feel twisted. Doesn't help that the ground beneath is so frigid and hard.

My throat. It… burns. Each breath hurts like it's all torn up.

I muster all that I have to give my legs a gentle twitch. A soft clanging of chains.

Of course.

I can feel now the weight of whatever's strapped around my ankles separately from the weight of my own legs. My ankles feel warm, moist. And they sting.

Stop ringing, I tell my head as if I could control it.

Stop. Ringing.

And its cloudy. So cloudy. I feel drugged, and it feels sickening. As if my mind is not of my own.

Somewhere, a door opens.

I try to turn my head towards that direction. It's taking so much effort just to move my head. And it hurts. It hurts so much. I can't help the tear that slowly drizzles down the side of my face.

I look up, and the Pig is there. Just staring. In his hand is a small lantern. It lights up the basement. I guess I'm in his basement.

Of course.

My clothes are still on. Just my boots are missing. Did he want me awake while he had his way with me?

Disgusting bastard. Garbage.

"Oh, you woke up." He seems surprised. "I went to go get a couple of more."

A couple more what?

"I thought you ruined my night." He speaks articulately with an accent of poise and elegance. But his voice is gruff and unfitting of his speech. A paradox. "But you made it better than I could have possibly imagined."

He takes a step and closes the door behind him.

My hands. I scrape the tips of my fingers against the cold stone tiles. My gloves are also missing. He saw it. He knows about it.

He walks down the steps with weight and steadiness. With each step, he shows me new parts of the basement while shrouding the rest back into darkness. The basement is surprisingly clean. I can see a table or sort across from me. He lights the candles on them. There are books. Parchments. And other things… stones. Pens. Ink. Hammer. Knife. Saw. Tools. My letter.

Oh God, the letter.

It looks still sealed. He didn't take a look at it yet. One saving grace.

"Don't worry. I won't… *violate* you," the Pig says. "That isn't what this is about. Though I have to say it's awfully tempting. You have very fair skin. And it'd be very… exotic to impregnate a woman from another world." He brushes the back of his hand down my cheek and body. He grabs my lips with his fingers and massages it. Like a cook checking the quality of meat.

I slap his hand away.

He chuckles.

"But women aren't my usual choice to... *satiate* my lust," he says.

I try to conjure something. The ringing in my head suddenly turns to a screech, and my entire body jolts as if someone just stabbed a nerve.

"I can't be distracted by using you for things that you're not to be used for." From the pockets of his dirty, patched pants, the Pig reveals two long needles. It has a twisted black metal as its "grip" and the rest of it the blade... the business end... is a long dark greenish crystal, needle-thin but thick enough to see its edges.

"Now hold still." His giant hand grabs around my cheeks and pulls me in. The Pig's strength is undeniable, and his grip feels like he'll tear my cheeks off. I try to struggle, but I feel weak. My hands can only gently slap and rub against his gargantuan forearms.

"You'll feel only a pinch," he says as I feel the tip of the needle tear through my scalp.

I scream. But not much of it makes it out through his grip.

It hurts, but as soon as he lets go of the needle, I feel numb. Cloudier than before. He lets go, and I fall to the cold, hard ground.

I'm reminded of the maiden.

At least she made it out.

I did what I set out to do.

That bitch.

I think I'm drooling. I'm not sure.

"There's one more." He picks me up again. I think he only let go to get some amusement out of me falling like a broken doll.

I can't even feel his grip anymore.

But the needle I could feel. As it tears through my scalp and pierces through my skull and brain, I could feel it all. It burns. I don't let out a scream but a shudder of sort.

He drops me again.

"Now, you'll eventually at least get to a point where your thoughts become coherent again." The Pig walks back to his worktable and sorts through his tools. He picks up a hammer. "And maybe it'd be a good idea for me to make sure that you won't be able to make much fuss."

The iron hammer dances in front of me. I can smell the metal. So close to my face, I can also see dried blood on it.

Do what you want.

Do your worst.

I won't even give you the satisfaction of hearing me scream.

"But I don't really see the point of it." The Pig retracts the hammer. "And I should really start preparing my dinner if I want to sleep on time."

He walks back and puts the hammer back on the table.

"Sleep well," he says as he blows out the candles on the table. "I'll bring you some food in the morning."

Everything feels like it's melting in a haze.

"When you're in a better mood for food that is."

With that last remark, I hear him walking away. The thick stomps up the stairs.

As the sound dwindles with each step, I feel relief.

Before the room descends into complete darkness once again, I study my insignia. I see a hole. His beating yesterday must have been more severe than I thought. A chunk of the insignia had been used up to heal my wounds. Perhaps whatever's left will be enough for me to recover from what he's done to me.

Rapid, scurrying stomps roar throughout the basement. The room brightens with light once again.

The Pigs snatches my hand away from me, puts my ring finger into his mouth and bites it off.

It all happened so quick that I didn't even realize what happened until I saw the blood spurting from where my finger used to be. I bring my hand into my chest and hold it tight.

I squealed, I think. I wasn't ready for it. I gave him the satisfaction.

He tears my hand away again from my grasp as he chews on my finger. The gnawing and crunches. I hope I'll be able to forget those noises. He shoves the stub that used to be my finger into the flames of his lantern.

I scream.

He lets go of the hand, and it collapses onto the cold, hard ground. I just let it be there.

"There you go," the Pig speaks kindly. Gently. "That'll keep it from going bad."

A loud, haunting swallow.

Leave me be.

Just leave me alone.

The Pig makes his way up the stairs again and closes the door behind him.

I'm only left with the darkness and the drips.

I bring my hand towards my chest again and hug it tight.

With any luck, I'll pass out.

Don't look at it, I tell myself.

Don't look at it.

But my fingers betray me, and I feel a stumpy, crusted stub where my finger used to be.

I scream once more.

***

Sometime during the night, I hear it.

"Hey... hey... hey..."

A voice. An androgynous voice calls out from the unknown beyond my part in the room. It sounds like it's in pain.

"Hey... Hey!" I'm happy that I'm not alone. And yet, immediately concerned by the idea of wondering how many more could be here... in the darkness. I must save him. I decided it's a him for now.

"Are you okay?" I call out to him.

He moans.

"What's your name?"

Silence.

"Hello?" I try to reach out to him again.

He suddenly gasps loudly and rapidly.

Before I can ask if he's okay, he starts to wail. A loud, almost violent wail.

As if my presence with him didn't give him hope but made him realize how much more hopeless our circumstances are.

What has he been through?

How long has he been here?

I want to tell him it'll be okay—even though I don't know if that'd be a lie or the truth. But I save my dwindling strength as I know he won't hear me.

"It'll be okay," I whisper anyway.

The wail… the sheer noise is traumatic.

I can't sleep.

In the darkness, it echoes not only in this abyss, but also in my mind. I'm not sure if I'd even be able to tell if he stops.

It's shaking my own consciousness. My own confidence. My sanity.

Tears are coming down my face, and I don't even know when it began. It pools by the side of my face before seeping into the stones. It's warm. The only warmth I feel.

I want to tell him to shut up.

My sympathy has run out.

But I don't have the strength.

And his wail has already pervaded my spirit.

The door opens.

"Alright, that's enough." The Pig appears. He speaks as if not out of annoyance, but as if he finally grew bored of it.

He walks off to the edge of the darkness beyond what I can see. I try to tilt my head to see him. My cellmate.

Hidden by the Pig's disgustingly thick and wide stature, I can only see his hands and fore arm. Stretched out like Jesus and his hands hanging on hooks.

Christ.

My cellmate shrieks at the Pig before resorting to panting like a dog in wet summer heat. He's tired.

The Pig grabs some sort of syringe and injects into the cellmate's stomach region. He grows quiet.

As the Pig turns around, he can see me, flat on the cobblestones, staring at him with my deadened eyes. He comes up close and places his fat, flabby hand on my face.

"Sorry about that," he whispers. "We'll get started on you soon."

I want to spit at his face.

Bite his fingers off.

Gouge out his eyes.

But I can't.

I just want him to leave.

Leave me in the darkness again.

Let me rest. Somehow forget this for even a few brief hours.

He leaves and closes the door behind him.

I lose consciousness again.

48

***

I'm not sure how long I spent in the darkness, but the Pig's "soon" doesn't seem so soon.

Time is swallowed by the darkness, and my moments awake and asleep all blend together.

I'm not even sure how long I'm asleep for, but it never feels enough.

Sometimes I wake up to the aches.

Sometimes I wake up simply because my mind won't allow me to sleep.

Sometimes I wake up to my cellmate calling out to me again.

"Hey… hey… hey…" he says.

"Hey," I say just as softly back to him. Part of me is still clinging on to the hope that he'd say more.

But he never does.

Sometimes he moans. Sometimes he seems to cry. But thankfully, I wonder at all if out of concern for me, he hasn't wailed again.

"How are you?" I ask sometimes when the loneliness becomes too much.

"How long have you been here?"

"Are you an Otherworlder as well?"

Maybe my questions are bit too inquisitive. Maybe he's too shy or too damaged to answer.

"Don't worry, we'll make it out. We'll make it through this."

"Hang in there."

I wonder if my one-sided conversations progressively became more about me than about communicating with him.

Has he forgotten me? Us?

Or maybe he died somewhere.

Good. I can live with the idea that I'll die here if he's dead as well.

I try to conjure any sort of magic again.

But whatever those needles are, they're still working. I counted four. Each points of entrance aches even still. Part of me is tempted to pull them out but even touching them shot up a shock through my nerves. The pain is nothing like anything I've felt before. I don't even have the strength to grip them. All I end up doing by trying to take them out is torturing myself.

Then I hear signs of life again.

Footsteps. Too many. He's not alone.

Laughter.

Luggage being set down.

And as time went by, the aroma of dinner. In my starvation, I can even pick apart what ingredients must be being used. Whoever prepared the meal, prepared a proper meal with different kinds of spices and meat.

Time passes by as I'm forced to listen and smell their dinner party.

Then a loud clash.

Probably someone is in a drunk stupor and fell.

Part of the floorboard chips, and a light shines

through.

By some miracle, it's right where I am. For the first time since who knows how long, I see the light. It's bright. It hurts my eyes. But I look up at it.

Someone's looking right at me.

Not the Pig.

But the drunk who fell over.

He can see me.

I can tell.

Through the small chip, his eye... I could see it widen.

He laughs and picks himself up.

He rejoins the festivities with the Pig again.

The Pig's loud, roaring laughter twists my insides.

Help me, you bastard.

Help me.

But at this point, I wouldn't be surprised if he was just another Pig in a different skin.

***

Stay awake.

Don't risk missing the chance of your rescue by sleeping.

Don't waste any time during the rescue by having him wake you up.

I count. I recite in my head my favorite movies. I

think of Loren, Tarron, and whomever else I met during my journey.

I remember mom and dad back home. And my brothers.

The door opens. But for once, it creaks open slowly.

Each step he took echoes in the darkness. Each creak probably frightening both of us that it'd wake up the Pig.

A gentle, greenish light is emanating from his body.

He is the angel to my prayers. My savior.

I hope.

Soon, he stands in front of me. He's tall. The light is emanating from a necklace around his neck. An artifact of sort. Short-ish hair. I can't really tell what color with the mix of green light and the darkness. But even in the darkness, I can see freckles. A lot of freckles on his perpetually squinting face. Bandages wrap around his head and covers his left eye.

"Help me," I whisper. "Please help me."

He looks around my body and picks up my hand. I think he's looking at my hand. The insignia. It has a bigger hole in its red filling than before.

"What happened to your finger?" He asks as he looks at the stub that used to be my ring finger. The cause of my insignia to wane further than it already was before.

"He ate it," I tell him.

"…Damn."

Yeah. '*Damn.*'

"Yeah, sure. I'll help," he says almost unenthusiastically. "You're from our world, huh?"

"Yes." I try not to break down. But hearing someone from home. I can't help myself. "Yes I am."

"Where you from?" he asks as he helps me sit and rest my back against a pillar.

"Britain," I tell him. "I'm from a small town called Hereford."

It's his necklace that is as bright as a torch. Bright enough to blind me. He's wearing an iron breastplate but red metal shoulders, greaves, and armband.

Why am I noticing all these details? Is it because this is the first person I've seen after all that time in the darkness?

He picks up my face gently and studies it. I feel a bit uncomfortable, but feel in no place to complain.

He smiles.

"Please help," I plead again.

"Of course, m'lady." He seems a bit happier about the idea now.

I chuckle at his cheesy jest. It's good to smile. It's good that I can feel what a smile is like.

"The man put something in my head," I tell him.

"I can see it," he says. "It's like antennas coming off of your head. There's like four."

"You're American?" I recognize his accent.

"Yeah, name's Jake," he says as he gently grabbed the tip of one of the needles. I felt my entire body jolt.

"Does it hurt?" He has an amused smile on his face. It creeps me out a bit.

"Yes." It felt as if someone had poked at the root of

rotten teeth. Entire nervous system going into shock. "My name is Camilla."

"Should I pull these out?" he asks with slight nervousness. He looks concerned now.

"I think those are keeping me from having any energy. I can't…" I gasp for air. "I can't cast any spells. I can't even move properly."

"You know how to cast spells?" He sounds surprised. I suddenly feel an immediate regret of sort in my gut. Not all of us Otherworlders can use spells. In fact, most of us can't. I'm the only one that I know of who can. I figure we just weren't bred to be able to cast spells. This isn't our world, after all. The insignia, in some sense, just evens out some odds.

As he pinched the tip of the needle, the pain jolts me again.

"If you move, I might end up breaking off a piece inside your brain," Jake says. Not to be funny. Not to scare me. But he sees it as a real possibility. Good motivation to stay still.

When he removed that first needle, I felt relief like I never felt before. But also a bit sore as it moistened with my blood.

He held it in front of him, a needle red with my blood about as long as a kitchen knife.

I feel uncomfortable staring at it. He tosses it aside.

As he removes the second, I can feel some energy coming back. The cloudiness of my mind slowly dissipating.

"What… what happened to your eye?" I ask to distract me from the pain.

"...Redtails," He says after a pause. "Redtails got me."

"And you survived?" I've heard of Redtails. There's small talk of him even amongst the Order and the royals. The one who hunted down the Otherworlders. People like Jake and I. Some think of him as a nuisance. Some think of him as a nuisance who's at least cleaning up a mess. Most of us, the Otherworlders, think of him as a traitor. A mass murderer.

"Yeah." He pinches the last needle.

It gives me confidence in my rescuer to hear that he survived Redtails. I don't think I've ever heard of a single survivor.

"Hey... Hey... Hey..." My cellmate calls out to me. I feel happier for him than I felt for myself that a rescue came for me.

"What was that?" Jake seems frightened.

"We have to rescue him. He's another victim," I tell him.

"Why?" He sounds so apathetic. So uncaring.

"We have to." I can't form any solid arguments. I'm too tired and in too much pain. Why do I have to explain this anyways? "We HAVE to."

Should we save a drowning child even if it means risking our chance to save ourselves?

He begrudgingly walks over to the other end of the darkness. Beyond the line I haven't crossed yet.

"Oh, shit!" Jake cries before he quickly remembers to lower his voice. "What the fuck?"

"What is it?" I'm trying to pick myself up but am having a hard time. My legs shake and wobble. I can't put any energy into them.

"I don't… I don't think he's coming with us," Jake says. "I don't think he can."

No. He's coming with us. He's coming with us, you bastard. I'm not going to leave anyone behind with that monster.

"Help me," I can't stand. "Help me!"

He's mesmerized by whatever it is he's staring at. He can't hear me.

I wobble my way. Taking one heavy and yet weak, painful step after another.

The letter.

I make my way to the table and grab the still unopened letter from Loren and stuff it deep into my pocket again. I hope I'm not too late.

Some energy slowly makes its way back and my legs actually feel like they belong to me once again. But each step is still heavy and painful.

I make my way to Jake.

Christ.

Just like how I remember him, my cellmate is stretched out against the wall. His hands and feet skewered through the four hooks. But he has no face. It's carved off above the lower jaw. His skin and muscle surgically lacerated and stretched open from his arms, legs, and torso to reveal all the inner workings of his body. Somehow, everything is still functioning. The heart's beating. Lungs inflating and deflating. And each time the hands twitch, you can see the muscles and the tendons in the arms flex.

But both of our attention was towards the lower part

of this man's torso.

A growth. A tumor of sort that stretched out from the lower intestines.

Its flesh spread all over in and out, throughout, the body like a web.

It's a face.

A skinless face.

It has eyes… eyeballs without lids looking at us.

It huffed and gasped for air.

And it groaned.

The familiar groan I've heard for so long.

"Is it… crying?" Jake asked. "Or is that just… blood or some shit?"

Something was drizzling down its eyes.

"Kill him." I didn't need to think too long to know how I could help my cellmate.

"What?"

"Just kill him!" I reached for his sword and almost tumbled back onto the hard ground. My one-eyed rescuer catches me.

"Alright." After he helps me stand and regain my balance, Jake draws his sword.

I look at my cellmate. His eyes roll around to look at me.

Sorry. I mouthed.

"Sorry," I say out loud after realizing he wouldn't be able to read the lips of a foreign language.

Jake quickly spins around, unsheathing his sword. A

loud clash echoes through the dark basement.

"Shit!" Jake yells.

I spin my head to see the Pig. He has a trident pointing toward us. He's smiling. I can't tell what the smile means. Is he simply confident? Or is he smiling at me facing what was certainly to be my own future?

Despite his impressive deflection, Jake seems worried.

"Ah, fuck. Fuck. Fuck!" Jake, though clearly distressed, gets into a stance for combat. "Come on, man! What the fuck is that?"

"You want to know?" the Pig asks with a slight hint of glee. "You know I liked working with you."

"Yeah, me too. So maybe we can all walk away," Jake suggests. I hope he means taking me with him as well.

"You see that jar next to him?" the Pig asks. There are rows of black, thick-shelled jars lined up next to my cellmate.

"Open one up," he suggests.

"Nah," Jake quickly answers. "I don't need to know more."

"Open it up, Jake," the Pig demands.

Jake slowly steps back and grabs onto the pot's lid. It's thick like the rest of the pots and from the looks of it, heavy. It takes a bit of effort from Jake to pull it off.

The stench from the jar bursts out, and it's rancid. I feel like throwing up, but Jake seems to have the stomach for it.

"What the fuck is that?" Jake says as he curiously stared into it. The Pig could have stabbed him at any moment.

"It's a person. A beautiful girl. I just put her in a more malleable form full of possibilities," the Pig explained. "And I'd like to give the two of you all the possibilities that she has."

"What is it?" I ask Jake as I covered my nose with my forearm.

Jake ignores me and looks at his hand. Checking his insignia. Desperate to see if it's filled so that he could escape. He looks serious. Ignoring his fear. It's fight or flight. I wonder if I can count on him to have me in the equation.

I concentrate.

Loren wouldn't give up.

Tarron wouldn't give up.

And I'm just not the type to give up.

My hand engulfs in white flame. A chaotic, unfocused form of magic. All I can manage for now.

A howl.

My cellmate is howling.

He rips through the hooks holding onto his hands and feet—losing a hand in the process—and lunges at the Pig. In his escape, he also shatters the jar that Jake opened, and a flood of red, putrid goo flushes out of it.

The Pig is caught by surprise.

I retch.

My cellmate's still howling with all of his anger and anguish.

I'm swept off my feet by Jake. He runs up the stairs.

I see the living quarters for the first time.

I can hear him howling still, and the stench of the goo still lingers by my nose.

It's disgustingly homely and warmly decorated. A burning hearth. A nice wooden table. Shelve of books.

The howling is silenced.

Jake kicks the door, but it doesn't budge.

The Pig runs up the stairs in a mess of blood and slime. I don't think any of that is his.

Jake kicks the door again, and it begins to crack.

I have to do my part.

I prepare a spell.

"The fire within us all. Whispers of Ark, the patron of carnage." I point the palm of my hand where the white flame still burns bright, asking for the gods of this world to lend me strength. *"Manifest."*

Crimson flame, the color of blood, spins out of my hand and hurls towards him like a serpent.

Burn, you bastard. Burn and die a slow death.

The Pig smacks away the flame with his trident. The crimson flame scatters all throughout his house and immediately immolates anything it touches into a hellfire.

Some of flame manages to catch the Pig but doesn't seem to stick.

My consciousness is barely holding on. But I must stay awake. I must live.

Outside, Jake's necklace begins to glow again.

We're in the woods. Of course.

It's the forest a decent way out of the town. The

trunks of each tree are at least the size of a small house, and they reach to the skies so high that I wouldn't be surprised if there were a whole world hidden among the leaves above.

At night, in the darkness, this forest is nightmarish. All the small rustles and signs of life. Knowing the next living thing could be a beast or a something far more nefarious and vicious to end your life horribly.

But right now, we only had one monster to worry about.

I can see him standing outside of his burning home. Huffing and puffing. He dashes towards us. Incredible speed for a man of his size.

"Shit." Jake can't seem to catch his breath. He weaves around different trees until he finally falls and drops me.

"Shit! Shit! Shit!" He cries.

I can't even feel the pain from the fall. My heart's pounding. I can't imagine his. The Pig is coming.

We can hear his mad stomps echoing in the woods.

The Pig is coming. He has stopped chasing. He's hunting now.

We hide behind one of the trees and rest our backs against it.

"I might actually have a chance if I had a full emblem." Jake stares at the back of his hand.

He turns his head towards me. He studies me in silence. As if he had an idea.

"Yo," he carefully says. The Pig's stomps growing louder and louder.

"Yes?" I'm breathing heavily. I can't be afraid.

Jake stands and draws his blade.

"You got any other spells left in ya?" he asks.

"No," I tell him. After the last spell, I'm powerless.

Jake seems determined. His mind seems made up.

"We're going to have to fight him." He raises his sword. Ready to strike.

"Agreed." I feel empowered by his courage.

"I want you to peek around the trunk for him," Jake suggests. "As soon as he's close, you let me know."

The plan doesn't make sense entirely. My gut feeling's uncomfortable with it. But I have to count on him for now. I sure hope he can end the Pig with a single strike.

I pray the strike to be true and vicious.

I turn my body around and poke my head out.

It's dark and silent.

But from a distance, I think I can see the glimmer of his trident.

I turn back around to check on Ja—

Episode 3
TAY'S CRATE

"…Happiness is just a word to me, and it might've meant a thing or two if I had known the difference," I sing to myself.

But even alone in the darkness, I'm self-conscious of my own singing. I'm a terrible singer. But it's still one of my few joys in life. Some people masturbate when they're alone to find relief from the harsh indifference of life, but I choose to sing. Most of the time anyways.

Then a thought comes to me. What if that old man could hear me while I'm in here. That stops my singing pretty quickly.

Does that make me petty?

A crack of light rips through the darkness.

About time.

Just fifty steps more. I counted last time. I wonder if it's the same this time. I had hoped I'd be able to check again someday.

Fifty-two. Fifty-two steps. Seems a reasonable margin of difference. Before I step into the light, I take a moment. It's not nervousness. It's not regret. It's just preparation.

I take the step forward. A weird sensation. There's a brief period where I feel nothing. Frightening nothingness that I've felt only once before. It's not even like being asleep. This is how death probably feels like. Even my consciousness pauses for a moment until my foot hits the ground on the other side.

It feels as if I only took a step, but in my memory there's a gap where everything is blank for a moment.

I feel the brown grass breaking beneath my feet. I'm in the fields of Mardosa. Gentle hills and grass plains toasted brown for the season.

The sun's setting.

The breeze just started to cool from the day's heat. This world sometimes feels too familiar to our own, and in many ways it is. There are just certain… quirks that makes it the 'Other'-world. I look at my elbow as it collects itself from its smoke-like state. My body is still forming.

Is a lucid dream better than a fleeting reality?

Am I just asking if a good fantasy is better than a bad truth?

Why am I being so… flowery?

I must be on my period.

Don't be an emo.

I see across the plains, down a couple notches of elevation, the town of Mardosa. It's a town parted in two by the river flowing through it. I think it's called the Si'ori River.

Maybe I should just run for it. A dash to the finish line. A safe zone.

My ears need to be free. They need to listen. Pay attention. I take off the earphones and wrap the cord around the player before putting it into my pocket.

And as if on cue, I hear them. Rustles in the grass. Heads poking out. From the looks on their faces, they look like hungry dogs seeing a bleeding raw meat for the first time in a long while.

One waves his hand at me. Three total. They try to mask their hunger and excitement. But they might as well have a hard-on seeing me from the look in their eyes. I'm being fucked.

"Hey! You new?" The bald man in his late 30s or early 40s approaches. About six feet tall. From his body, he probably hit the gym regularly back home. Not weight training. Calisthenics. He's speaking French, but I can understand him just fine. The stamp the gatekeeper gives us grants us a few perks.

A brown man behind him. An Indian? Middle-Eastern? Short. Probably about five-foot-six. Goatee that reminds me of either Satan or a 70s porn star. Doesn't seem like much.

And then the third man. "Man." Maybe in college. Maybe younger. Looks dumb. And zits. A lot of zits. Not the face you want to think of when you think of the phrases "our future" or "my child." About five-foot-ten. Fit-ish.

They look at one another to ascertain and agree upon my 'newness.' They feel pretty confident that I am. Can't blame them. I look the part. Most people would have had their gear on at this point, formed with their bodies as they entered the Otherworld. I put my hand with the stamp into my pocket. Let's see how all this plays out.

"Hey! Don't be afraid!" He shows his gloved hands to me. His two companions follow. They are also gloved.

These guys have been past Mardosa enough to run into a couple of places where they're not friendly towards the Otherworlders—us. Or maybe they're hiding their stamps from people of our own kind. There are a few reasons for that.

One of them—the brown one—quickly takes his gloves off and shows me his hand. His stamp is on his right hand. Only the red outline of the stamp is visible.

These dumbasses really do think I'm new.

These opportunistic, shit-guzzling, bottom feeders.

Preying on the weak. Using survival of the fittest as

70

an excuse. Natural selection as a punchline.

Garbage.

Utter trash.

I say nothing.

I pick up my pace and walk away.

"Don't be scared! We can help you! This isn't a game! You're in real trouble if you just walk out there," the bald man speaks.

"Yeah, there are monsters and magic and shit!" the bright-future-of-our-world cries after my growing shadow.

The tiny, mystery-in-origin brown man looks at the kid begrudgingly.

I'd show them my stamp. The hole in the center would tell them that my cherry's already been popped. But it'd also tell them that I'm an even more nutritious meal than they expected.

"No thanks," I tell them. "I kind of want to experience this on my own."

The bald man, in his mixture of dress shirt, pants, jacket, with a breast plate and leg plates, manages to find his sword and draws it.

It's an unremarkable blade. Iron blade. Sells for around twenty Zens or two-thousand Donos. Five Zens short of a single Qu. In that state, it'll probably sell for more like fifteen Zens. I could clean it up and probably sell it around this region for seventeen or hold onto it and head over to the Hig'Lor Mountains for back to around twenty Zs.

Then again, if I were to make the trip to the mountains, I'd be better off carrying herbs and roots from this region for the weight and space the sword would take.

71

"What are you trying to do with that?" I ask the bald man.

He says nothing and simply approaches me. The other two follows. The shorter brown man draws a sword of his own. The I'm-proud-of-my-1500-on-my-SAT draws two knives and holds them backwards. Of course he does. He even hunches over a bit as if he's a veteran assassin hidden behind the mask of skin complexion and the unspectacular future glazing over his eyes.

They don't look like hungry dogs anymore. They're hounds. Hounds ready to do whatever it takes to make sure their meal doesn't get away.

These boys need Jesus in their lives.

But I'm not sure if I'm someone who can deliver him to them.

Oh well.

If I die, I die.

But, then again, dying like sack of shit to a bunch of thieving thugs isn't the way I want to go right now. Depending on the way I look at it, I do have some responsibilities. Though, me leaving my gear behind here was precisely to deter me from coming back since these things could happen.

And of course, it happens.

Maybe I'm the one who needs Jesus. But as far as I know, he's not really known for showing up on time.

"Look," I step back slowly. I'm about three steps ahead from being in range of their weapons. Two of them start to spread apart from the bald man and begin to surround me. "I have—"

"Stop criminals!" I hear the voice of a young man

shouting towards us.

Jesus?

From the hills, a head appeared with a buzz cut and the colors of the tanned grass fields. A scrunched up face with freckles generously sprinkled between his eyes and lips. Looks to be about 18 to maybe 20 years of age. Athletic build. About six foot in height. He has a deep crimson breast plate with shoulders, gauntlets, leggings, and greaves to match. A full set of sort—can't recognize where it might be from. With the leather boots and the bag strapped around his back, this kid adapted to this place and survived. Maybe even thrived. He already has his sword drawn. It's a well-crafted blade. Silver, rectangular cross guard, black grip, with a pointed pommel that you can probably smash a helm with. There are embedded red and green stones in the pommel. Wonder what those are. With gentle engravings that could be a sign of enchantments, this sword could be worth easily ten to thirty Qus.

My savior. My red knight in shining armor. My hero.

But the reality is, he very well could be another opportunist. Is a robber of robbers truly a friend of mine? If he isn't, then I have a much scarier robber on my hands.

Not Jesus. I'm not that lucky. Maybe the other guy. Lucifer.

Or worse. Neither.

"Damn it, it's Jake," the short brown man speaks. I think it's definitely Arabic. But I don't even know if they have different dialects and totally different languages in the Middle East. I should look into this somehow. I feel a bit embarrassed. For all I know he could still be Indian speaking Indian. What do they speak there again? Punjabi?

"Robbing newbies?" Jake takes a step and they all

take a step back. "I thought y'all had your fill last time."

Poor guy or gal. Hope it was quick.

"That was only enough for me." The bald man peeled off his gloves to show his stamp. Filled. Completely red.

The last of the trio, we-all-got-trophies-for-trying, reveals his hand. He only has a red outline of the stamp.

They had it rough out there.

Fuckers.

"And y'all pussies are too afraid to go out there and earn it." Jake waves his sword in front of them like a teacher waving a pointer.

"They can kill you to grow stronger and to fill up their symbols," Jake turns to inform me. "Just so you know."

I know. But I say nothing. Better to play along this me being a damsel in distress thing.

"If we go out there again like this, we'll die," the ambiguous-in-race man speaks. "We can't even go home like this."

I have a feeling these aren't the type of guys who'd go home if they did finally refill their stamps. It feels like believing in gamblers who tell you they'll go home once they break even.

"I don't want to go home," the brighter-tomorrow contests.

The shorter man simply groans and doesn't say anything.

"Why not the two of you just kill Remi?" Jake points his sword at the startled baldie.

They all look at one another silently.

"Look at that!" Jake says excitedly. "Sebastian is actually considering it!"

Sebastian, the kid, looks dumbly at Jake and back at Remi. He doesn't even realize Jake might have just sealed one of their fates today.

And they've all forgotten me. It's a good time to walk.

I walk away.

"Stop!" Jake yells after me.

And I listen. What else can I do?

"Show me you hand!" He demands.

Son of a bitch.

Rat faced, shit-eating, piece of dog shit.

Asshole.

I comply.

"Oh, look at that." Jake walks up and grabs my wrist for closer inspection. "This guy's been here before. I'm guessing he came back to Mardosa because he has a crate with the bank in town, right?"

Bastard. The kid's a bit smarter than I thought. I keep my poker face.

He looks back at the three stooges and nearly drags me along towards them.

He's strong. Not just enhanced by the stamp, but strong. Definitely had his time here. Maybe it's his armor.

"Here's the deal," Jake says. "I'm sure you got some cash stashed up to have a crate. Offer me some protection money, or I'll let these guys have at you."

"...How do you know I just won't pay?" I felt dumb

as soon as that question finished coming out of my mouth.

"Because then you have me to deal with," Jake correctly answers.

"Fine. Twenty Zens." I think it's a reasonable amount. A good number start with. Obviously not a number worth my life, but let's see how big this kid's stomach is.

"Yo. You okay being my bitch until you fill up till a Qu?"

"Fine, one Qu."

"You have one Qu?"

"At the bank." I do. It's a good chunk of money but nothing I can't afford. Better than dealing with this shit. Just get this over with. Don't have a lot to bargain with.

"If you're fucking with me, you know I'll kill you, right?" I think he wanted to sound tough and menacing, but he just comes off as a douche.

"Sure."

"You hear that guys? This guy—" Jake puts his arm around me. "—what's your name, man?"

"Tay."

"Tay? Is that a real name? You kind of seem like a guy who'd use like a screenname for this," Jake questions.

"It's my real name."

"What's your last name?" Jake asks too much.

"Go fuck yourself," I tell him.

"Alright guys…" Jake faces the stooges again. "…Tay Go Fuck Yourself is under my protection now."

"Fuck you, Jake," Remi says. "You know how long

we've been waiting for another newbie to roll around these parts?"

"I'm sick of his shit." The brown man approaches Jake with his blade. "You motherless, ball-less cowards can either watch or help me take both of these guys down.

"Hey man," Jake says. "I don't like killing our own people."

But we all knew the fight was already inescapable. Jake releases me from his arm and slowly approaches the brown man.

"What's your name?" Jake asks with an almost mocking smile. "I never got your name."

"Fuck your sister," Fuck Your Sister answers.

"Weird names y'all have." Jake thinks he's hilarious.

It isn't that Jake is a remarkable or a notable fighter. I've seen many better. It's possible in this world he might get around further than many simply due to his stamp and its perks. But he's slightly above average at best. His confidence in himself, however, perhaps is phenomenal. A cheap steroid to one's talents that's perhaps poison to growth. Maybe as time goes on that confidence, the stamp, and experience will form an atomic bomb of a concoction that this world will have to deal with.

Who knows. Only Sarne. Or maybe not even him.

But the point is that while Jake is above average, Fuck Your Sister is a terrible fighter. Never mind that he was dumb enough to pick a fight with an empty stamp. It feels like watching an accountant holding their sword for the first time. Fighting for his life for the first time. How long was he out here until he used up his stamp? Was he just living off Remi's back? He probably didn't even realize what all that meant until Jake's sword was pushing through his chest. You can always tell who wasn't ready for their deaths by how surprised they look when they are dealt the fatal blow.

What made you think you were immune from dying, Fuck Your Sister? Even a church collapses every once in a while on a prayer circle. We all die. Don't look so surprised. Don't look as if you feel that you didn't deserves this. No one gets what they deserve.

If Jake was a better fighter, he probably could have ended it without killing the man. Not sure if Jake even knows that. He looks proud. The man's blood is noticeable even on his red armor.

I kind of hoped at least one of the two stooges left would cry after the man's name, but neither of them did. They simply stared at the dying man without much remorse as if the expected happened.

"We're done here, right?" Jake asks as he shakes off the blood from his sword.

The two men quietly approached the dying man's body and began patting around his pockets and relieving him of his gear as he was still taking his last breaths.

"Hey!" Jake yells at them. "Fuck off!"

They look disgruntled, but they comply. Watching someone kill their friend can have that effect on people.

"One day, Jake. One day." Remi points at Jake.

"Yeah, maybe one day I'll fuck you up too," Jake replies as he digs through the body of the man who's still very much alive.

Fuck Your Sister is at this point crying. Saying a prayer of sort. Apologizing to a lot of people. As Jake shoves his hand up his pants to see if the dying man is hiding anything. His friends are already turning around and getting ready to walk off.

Get ripped to pieces out there, fuckers.

I think the man's dead. He's quiet now. His chest stopped bobbing up and down.

Jake finds some money and puts it in his pocket. I counted about seventy-eight Donos. He hands me the dead man's sword, sheath, and pouches.

I accept my role as the mule for the trip back to town.

"What did you mean you don't like killing our people?" I ask as we embark on our journey to town. The wind is colder now. But I enjoy listening to the grass field rustle in the breeze.

"What?" He replies dumbly.

"You don't mind killing the people here?"

"I mean, I've killed the people here before—y'know, like the bad ones," Jake answers. He almost sounds like it's a burden to answer. I'm hassling him. "But killing people from our world… just feels wrong. It feels like murder."

How did he figure? I worry and wonder.

"What's the difference?"

"What do you mean, what's the difference?" Irritation makes him sound a bit more awake. "This world's like a game, you know? It's not real—"

"This isn't a game," I tell him.

"I mean, I know that, but you know what I mean? It doesn't feeeeel real to us. Besides, how do you know that you know for sure this place is real anyways?" Even more irritated now. Perhaps it's not wise for me to push him too much.

I wondered once. It's a common illness people from

79

our world have when we get here.

"But it is real," I assure him. Then again. Do I really know for sure myself?

How much does it matter whether or not I can conclude that this is real life or just fantasy?

Caught in a landslide.

No escape from reality.

Wonder if this is what that meant.

Probably not.

"Even then, ain't our laws. Ain't our world." Jake pauses for a moment, and we walk in silence. "Shut the fuck up, man. Grown ass man who had to be saved. Don't you have kids you should be raising anyways?"

"Yeah." Why did I answer that? "No. Not exactly."

"What kind of a fucking answer is that?" He sounds pissed. "You a dead beat dad or something? I thought Asians were supposed to be the good ones."

It was an honest answer. I guess it's still a debate in my mind. I never did resolve it.

Fuck.

But fuck you, Jake.

"Man, poor girl whoever it is you knocked up," Jake goes on. "But she must be a dumb bitch to be with a guy who'd fuck her over like that."

Because the world works that way, right, kid?

Because you, in your great wisdom of being alive for maybe two decades figured all this shit out, right, kid?

Or maybe it does. And we get older and we just clutter shit in our lives and think of them as legitimate excuses.

"Shut the fuck up," I say something.

And then I say nothing.

Fucking Jake.

***

"So that's all you did? Like business kind of stuff?" Jake confirms.

"Yeah, I focused a lot of my time making money. It was fun to see how things I've learned in our world still applied here. Got to travel a bit and meet interesting people," I tell him. I seem to have earned some of his confidence and respect. "Money opens doors anywhere and everywhere."

"Yeah," Jake agrees. "It ain't power, though. I want power. And money. But power."

Indeed.

"So you are a business man back home?" Jake asks.

"No, I mean, not really. Not exactly."

"What's with you and these weird-ass, half-assed answers?" Jake seems annoyed.

I'm lawyer. I worked for a big firm for a little while but then decided I wanted to do something on my own. Thought I was young enough to try, but didn't realize how old I'd feel if I failed. If things had worked out, it would have been a great, adventurous, young-guy-making-it story. It didn't.

I don't want to tell you, Jake, not only because I don't

have to tell you shit, but also because I don't really want us to have any more connections beyond whatever happens here.

"By the way, man..." Jake asks as we walk through the town square of Mardosa. "...you high or something? You seem to just fade away. I'll take weed as payment if you got some. I kind of don't like what they get high off of here."

To Jake's credit, I've heard that before. I do 'fade away' a lot.

"Sorry, no weed. Money will have to do," I let him know.

We receive a lot of nods and waves from the people we've made eye contact with as we moved through the city. We don't know them. They're strangers. But people in general in this world are... nicer. Friendlier. A bit more naive. In a sense, life is the same anywhere, but most people in this world are exposed to a lot less. Things are simpler.

We are the corruption. We are the disease. Not a disease that wouldn't have happened without us, but we're...accelerating the process. At least that's how I feel from time to time.

But I still marvel at how pretty Mardosa is. Still the pretty town that I remembered it as. I remember being mesmerized by it when I first came here. It reminds me a lot of Europe with a hint of Asia. Even with the bit of the cluttered feeling. Most of the buildings here are at least two floors. Usually the bottom floor is used for business while the top is for living quarters. One large bridge connects the two towns together. You'll often see small boats going up and down the river for people who wants to travel quickly.

It's a bigger town than most out there. A town neutral to the Otherworlders, at least for now, and not really caught up in the political power struggle between the royals and the king. One of the few large towns in the kingdom of Lynark without a royal attached to it. It's controlled by three rich families who made their fortunes through hard work and trade.

The town is relatively young, but grew extremely quickly. One of the few towns that I actually know shit about.

But the cynical bastard in me wonders: how long until one of the rich families claims royalty and then pursues controlling this town? How long until this town seems tempting enough for the king or the other royals?

I bet within the next decade. At the latest, by the time the kids are old enough.

But that's why I like their banking guild.

They remain independent, and even the powerful pushes to keep them that way. They serve all kinds and any kind that'll pay their fees and bring their investments to life. That has its own problems, but for most of their customers, it's a good thing in a world that can be turned inside out by political instability.

We stand in front of a large, sturdy-looking building that looks like it was carved out of stone. Above its thick, heavy, wooden doors is a giant symbol of the banking guild made of steel and a single jewel. A simple blue square jewel in a silver circle.

I'm choosing to ignore that the work they're doing above their building seems to be more repairs than remodeling.

I am unlucky. But come on.

We walk in and through the aisle of columns.
The security used by the Banking guilds have quite the
reputation. Some claimed they're trained well enough to
rival the kingdom's elites. They all wear the same uniform
of blue robes tinted with silver and all carry a long, steel
staff as their standard weapon.

I hear the elite members in their ranks can even use
sorcery.

Another reason why I love this bank.

There seems to be more security than usual though.

My luck can't be that bad.

"Something seems off," Jake says.

Shut the fuck up, Jake.

We reach the counter. Behind the golden fence he
hides behind, Mr. Lor recognizes me and his face turns to a
grimace.

"Mr. Tay," he says with a sinking heart. His and
mine.

No one knows my last name. I like it that way.

"I'm so sorry, sir," Mr. Lor says.

"What happened?" I ask.

"We…" Mr. Lor seems ashamed. Embarrassed. He
lowers his voice to a whisper. "We were robbed."

"God damn it!" Jake's loud voice echoes through the
halls. He's pretty quick for a turd.

"So what does that mean?"

"They seemed to have been specifically targeting
the blue and black crates. It was an elaborate plan. The
most elaborate plan I've ever heard of or witnessed. And

I've heard of and witnessed all kinds, sir. These were professionals. But don't be concerned—so are we. We are the banking guild, after all! This will be a one-time thing. Yes, indeed, they won't be able to do such a thing again. Oh, no, no, no sir! So don't be concerned about doing business with us. We are, indeed, still, and always will be, the very best of the best."

Through all the gibberish Mr. Lor was giving me to defend his and the bank's honor, I know Jake only heard: Blue. Crate. Black. Crate.

His ears are burning red. He's trying his best to hide his excitement. And somewhere in there is an evil hamster hopped up on cocaine running on the wheel trying to figure out a way to siphon more money out of me by turning my misfortunes into his fortune.

I know it'll disappoint him a bit, but I'm a blue crate. The blue crates were reserved for people who were just a step below the most valued clientele—the black crates. Certain thresholds of wealth had to be met before you were even qualified for the qualifications.

It was a rigorous and sometimes even a demeaning process. But the perks. Oh, the perks. I've only felt slighted by the bank when the black crates get involved. I need my crate. But the Azure Guards will be focusing on the black crates.

"The Azure Guards were able to stop them before they took too many of them but it seems they unfortunately got yours. Unfortunate, yes. Sir, it was quite unfortunate. You were quite unlucky," Mr. Lor continues.

I wait for it. Mr. Lor has a bad habit of saying things that didn't need to be said, but he usually makes up for it. I take his bad habit as a sign of his honesty.

"But of course, we are here to make sure even the

most unlucky customers feel the most secure and fortunate when they are with us so your losses will be covered by our banks as soon as we have… all our ducks in order…"

"Which means?"

"In the case we cannot retrieve your crate, we'll need to confirm your loss with you and verify how you'll receive your payment, and within two peaks to a turn we will be able reimburse you." Mr. Lor looks nervous. Two peaks to a turn. That's either a little less than two weeks or a little more than a month. "But that's after the investigation is over. For now, we can just start the process to give you temporary funds. But given the… circumstances involved…"

He means black crates. They get priority.

"…and the funds that need to be reimbursed, we'll need some time to figure all of it out." It's rare when Mr. Lor disappoints me.

"What… what did he have?" Jake asks.

He's salivating. Can't contain his excitement, I guess.

"Well…" Mr. Lor looks at me for permission.

"Let's do a cursory reminder," I say. Though it's unnecessary, it might be good to assure Jake and also keep him in line.

"Well, sir, you didn't keep much." Mr. Lor quickly pulls out the paper from a short stack. There aren't many of us blue crates.

Jake seems slightly disappointed.

"A helm."

I nod.

"A weapon."

I nod.

"Maps and parchments."

I nod.

"And a sum of…" Mr. Lor clears his throat. "Two Shura and fifty-two Qus."

Jake beady little eyes widen.

It's enough to buy a house.

"And to assure you, sir, your other crates in the other branches should be safe."

"Thanks." But this is the crate that I need. Not to mention I can't afford to go to the other branches.

"Who did this?" Jake asks.

Mr. Lor looks around and leans in.

"It's a bit of an interesting case. A group of unlikely alliances is what they're saying. I suppose money can bring all kinds together." Mr. Lor lowers his voice ever more. "Our own Azure Guards investigations have shown that the notorious Redtails was involved somehow."

Redtails?

"Yo. See? More reasons for me to get that bastard," Jake turns and tells me.

"Are the birds available?" I ask Mr. Lor.

My question startles him.

"Sir, you're not possibly thinking of?" Mr. Lor glances at Jake. "I mean, your friend seems capable, but I don't think even he…"

Mr. Lor clears his throat.

"We know for a fact some of the stash went with the Todo brothers. The Todo brothers, sir."

"Shit, you have some shitty luck," Jake remarks.

"Indeed," Mr. Lor chimes along.

I look at both of them. But I can't help but whole-heartedly agree.

Todo brothers. They are beastmen part-time mercenary and part-time thugs. Beastmen of the amphibian kind. I've only caught a glimpse of them once guarding some businessman in the tropical lands of Sor'soa.

They were around three meters tall. Rough, coarse desert toad-like skins. Long, muscular arms. A distinctive short horn… more like a calloused mold of skin between their eyes. From what I saw of them they were quiet, but I hear with a little drink they became like drunken sailors at a port after a tour.

"I've seen them before. Took down a giant basilisk by themselves. They were with a group of I think twelve others hired to take it down. The group even had a sorcerer," Jake shares an unrequested anecdote. "The Todo's waited for the twelve to be slaughtered before they took it down by themselves."

"What were you doing?" I ask.

"Wanted to enjoy the show. Maybe scavenge a little afterwards," Jake answers without hesitation.

Mr. Lor glances at me with a judging look for the company I keep around.

He clears his throat again.

"It'd require our more… elite… members of the Azure Guards to deal with the Todo brothers, sir. We are just running a little short on manpower at the moment with the investigation. The black crate members are… more pushy and influential if you understand…"

Redtails and Todo brothers. Something doesn't seem right.

I want my chest. I need my chest. I don't want it falling into the wrong hands. But knowing what kind of clientele black crates are, this is going to be messy. They were willing to ruffle the feathers of royals and other powerful people.

"Mr. Lor, I'll take the bird," I demand.

"Sir, I can't advise you to do that, but if you wish I can't stop you either." Mr. Lor looks worried. Sincerely worried.

"What's this bird that you're talking about?" Jake asks.

I nod to Mr. Lor. My mind is made up.

Mr. Lor places on the counter a small stone statue of a bird. It always reminded me of a raven with ornamental feathers on its forehead.

"Here's the ring," Mr. Lor says as he gives me a small ring with a purple jewel.

I put it on and life breathes into the small statue. The bird gently stretches its wings, revealing each of its ashy feathers and shakes its head. Its eyes are purple like the ring. It's stone no more and flesh and blood like any other bird.

Mr. Lor opens a small locked chest and feeds the bird a small blue stone.

"The bird will be now be locked onto your chest," Mr. Lor says. He then hands me a small crest the size of my palm with the bank guild's symbol. "And your key."

I put it in my pocket.

"So, you going on your own?" Jake asks as he plays

with the bird with his finger.

"I can't pay you unless we get to my chest. You don't have to come with me if you don't want. Just stick around Mardosa. I'll find you."

"Yeah, if you die then it becomes a problem, don't it?" Jake sounds disgruntled but still plays with the bird.

"I need my crate." I motion the bird over, and it lands on my shoulder.

"Yo, that's your problem." Jake seems a bit unhappy I took the bird. "I don't mind just holding you here until the bank takes care of your reimbursement. Don't forget who's whose bitch here."

Swallow it, Tay. He can be useful.

"Then come with me. I'll throw in fifteen Qus." Lowball offer. But this kid is hungry for money.

"Twenty-five Qus," he counteroffers. "Killing the Todo brothers will probably be good for my rep anyways."

First Redtails, and now the Todo brothers. Wonder if he's confident, a fool, or has a scheme. Maybe a little of all of the above.

"Done." Regardless, another Otherworlder coming with me will probably help my chances. I can afford the money.

"I'll signal the bird once it reaches its destination," I say, trying to ease Mr. Lor's concerns. "There's a chance the Todo brothers aren't involved with my chest at all."

"With your luck?" Jake points out.

I say nothing.

The bird senses my wishes and flies onto my hand.

"Roost," I command.

It closes up its wings and buries its head inside. It's stone again.

"Can I borrow a bag?" I ask Mr. Lor.

He looks a bit confounded by the request but finds me a knapsack somewhere.

We decide to spend the evening at Mardosa. Jake said it was his treat. His customer service. We went to a cheap inn. I strangely didn't feel like a whore even when he opened the door for me and offered to pay for dinner.

I've been to this inn before. They had decent food. Their specialty was this whole roast of a creature they called Polu—a mammal the size of a pig with the face of a rabbit, folded ears of a horse, and a body of a rat.

Fuck-ing delicious. At least however they made it here. If Jake wasn't going to pay for my own room, he was at least buying me my favorite meal.

Much like everywhere else in this town, it was separated into two floors. The first floor had a dining area, and I'm assuming in the back somewhere were the sleeping quarters of the owners. The second floor was for the guests. A lot of people in the town came here just to eat. Also a lot of kids, lonely husbands, and neglected wives came here for the upstairs. Some things don't matter which world you're in.

Glasses of water. A toasted bun with a gently thin, crispy crust on the outside and an unimaginably airy and soft inside. We wait for the entree.

"So what's your endgame here?" I ask Jake. "What are exactly planning to do?"

"With you?" He asks as he tears apart the bun into small chunks onto his plate. His hand then hovers over the chunks like one of those claw machines at the arcades as he chooses which chunk toeat first.

Just eat the damn bread like a normal, regular human being.

"No, with this world," I clarify.

"I don't know. I might kind of just live here." Jake chooses one and shoves it in his mouth. "Right now, specifically, I'm trying to kill that Redtails guy."

"Redtails?"

"You don't know him? The guy in black armor supposedly hunting down the people with emblems." He chooses his next pasty victim.

"Yeah, why him? Did he get someone you know?"

"Because he seems like a dick, and killing him will y'know… make me famous or some shit," Jake answers. "And I just want to see if I can do it."

"How do you plan to do that?" I ask. "You that confident in your skills?"

Jake smirks and studies me for a bit. Then he leans in.

"I got a trump card up my sleeve," he whispers.

He then chuckles.

"The armor?" I ask him. It's probably enchanted.

"Nah," he says.

The cocksucker studies me again with a smirk. He's trying to decide whether to open up or not.

"I got some special bombs just for him. Got it during a job in the Ocerion jungles."

A bomb, huh?

"Is that really worth risking your life for?"

"Yo. You can't be such a pussy, man. I just go with it, y'know? Do what I want. Get what I want. Deal with whatever that comes with doing exactly that."

I'm not sure why I don't have a reply to that. It's a childish, selfish, and a dangerous way to live.

Before I can inquire into more of his life, the roast comes out and the topic of conversation quickly changes to the cuisine of this world and what we miss from our own.

Soon afterward, we retire to our room to sleep. Both of us were possessive enough of the bed to not relinquish it to the other. So we decide to share it. I can see how uncomfortable Jake is with anything that may seem homosexual. But his stubbornness beats out his fear.

Jake snores. His victory. Maybe I'll spoon him.

As I stare at the wooden ceiling, it suddenly hits me that I'm spending my first night back at the Otherworld.

***

Jake is in a grumpy mood. He wants to eat. I'm still full from the roast before, but he's young. Always starving. The few pieces of bread and dried meat we grabbed on our way out of town aren't enough for his appetite.

The bird flies steadily. I hope they didn't make it too far.

Or maybe he's grumpy by the fact that I dictated over this morning's schedule.

Couldn't help it. Woke up with a slight panic attack and felt like I was wasting too much time. I have to get to my crate.

The bird led us out of Mardosa, back out onto the fields, and then into the Ien'dor Woods. There's a path, but as far as I know there's really nothing in this direction for miles. Countryside with a few farming villages here and there. Secluded. Dangerous with bandits, beasts, fiends, and the unknown. I guess the exact kind of crowd that we're looking for.

I start up a conversation to lighten his mood a bit. I ask about him. No. Be honest; I'm bored, and I'm curious about the kid.

He tells me he's in the military.

"I enlisted right after high school. Wasn't really sure what I was going to do. Military seemed fun. War seemed cool."

"Did you go to war?" I'm a bit surprised this kid was in the military at all. Doesn't seem the type. Doesn't seem like the kind of a person who can take orders for too long. Have his life dictated by others. Like this morning.

"Yeah."

"How was it?" I kind of feel like a kid asking. It's not like I haven't met veterans before.

"Some parts of it sucked. Some parts of it were fun. A lot of assholes in the military."

I wonder what kinds of people Jake would consider to be assholes. Regardless, I do the math in my head.

"Then, are you still in the military? You can't be done with your contract yet," I ask.

"I've been out." Jake shrugs.

"How?"

He shrugs again.

"Eh, don't ask. You don't tell me some shit, I don't tell you some shit. Like what's the deal with you and your kids?" Classic you-bring-shit-up-I-don't-want-to-talk-about-I-bring-shit-up-you-don't-want-to-talk-about.

"I don't have any kids," I tell him.

"You knocked up a girl, didn't you?"

"…I… well…"

Our conversation is interrupted by a woman sitting on the side of the path. She's in a dirty, olive green robe wrapped in belt of leather pouches. Her thin, silver hair spilled out beneath her hood. She's staring at us with big wide eyes. Curious, yet nervous.

In her hand is an unremarkable wooden staff that would look more like a worn out walking stick if it weren't for the tiny glyph at its tip. I can barely see it. It looks as ancient as her.

Jake scrunches up his face at the sight of her. He looks displeased. Disgusted even.

As we walk past her, she grabs my hand.

"Hands off, grandma," Jake says.

She's staring into my eyes. Pleading with me to give her a moment.

I crouch down.

"Yo, come on man," Jake complains. "You a sucker for this kind of shit?"

I kind of am a sucker for old people in need.

I don't speak, but simply observe her. Letting her know it's okay to say her piece.

Her fingers are long and tattooed with letters I don't recognize. Pretty sure it's not of this world and definitely sure it's not of our world. On the back of her spotted hand is a glyph of sorts, and I could see something similar in her palm. She points with her finger with their long, calcified, dirty fingernails at herself. And then at me. And then down the road.

She wants us to accompany her to the next town.

Before I answer, I glance at her other hand. It's clean from tattoos and is actually quite well kept. All fingers, however, are accessorized with elaborate rings each with different colored jewels.

They are either worth a fortune or nothing.

Come on, Tay. Not the time nor the place.

But seriously. That ring on her pinky definitely looks like it's worth something.

"Jake, she's coming with us," I tell him. I am a softie for old people.

"Hell fuckin' no!" he snaps. "You think you're going to feel any better dumping her somewhere than not picking her up here? Besides, how would we look travelling with a crippled old woman."

"I'll throw a bit more in my payment," I tell him.

"How much more?" he immediately asks. I kind of wonder if he's throwing a hissy fit just to get paid.

"Twenty Zens just to take her with us to the next town," I answer.

"Twenty-five," he counters.

"Twenty," I repeat my offer.

"Fine," he concedes. He underestimates how much I want to help this woman.

I offer the old lady my hand to help her stand. She

smiles and accepts with her tattooed hand. Her hand is extremely rough and calloused.

"Let's go," I tell her with a smile.

The old lady seems thankful. She digs through one of the many pouches dangling on her robe and hands me a small medallion. I suppose it's a thank you gift.

It's a platinum-like material with a deep crimson jewel that's shaped like a bird in flight embedded into it. I've seen this before. I turn and study her face. Her eyes widened and her lips stretched into a smile. She's wondering if I'm appreciating her gift. Her gratitude.

"I can't accept this." I try to smile warmly. My heart sinks a little when I see the disappointment and confusion wash over her face.

"Then give me that so I can sell it," Jake says. "Shit ain't yours to give back. You guys are under my protection, right?"

She looks agitated by Jake.

"Miss…" I stop walking and face her. "Maybe you can just give me a hug or something."

"Yo, you just going to ignore me now?" Jake complains.

The old woman doesn't even seem to hear Jake. She studies my face and thinks over my offer. She smiles. I smile back. She embraces me into a hug. She smells like roots, mold, and earth. I embrace her back.

I don't get compassionate for many things. It just isn't in my nature. I think that, actually, most of us lose that as we get older. It becomes a hindrance of sort. We save it for the people that matter in our own little worlds and lives.

The medallion with the crimson bird. I've seen it once before at a trade auction. It was apparently given to the few heroes by a late king of a kingdom long gone. Given to them for standing by their king until the kingdom's end. They left such an impression on the conqueror that he allowed the soon-to-be dethroned king to carry out the ceremony to award them.

This crippled, broken old woman was once one of the greatest heroes her time had ever known. Or maybe she had just picked it up somewhere. Who knows. What's a relic in a collection of junk? What's junk in a collection of someone who cherishs them all?

Still junk, I guess.

***

Neither Jake nor I have a clue where the path leads. We know there's a mountain region of sorts at some point from the map Mr. Lor showed us. Jake didn't want to pay for a map. He said it was unnecessary when we have the bird already. I feel as if there's a lost sense of importance for a physical map with the GPS generation. Mr. Lor warned us that if the bird led us that far, it would mean, more than likely, we were going to run into the Todo brothers.

I'll worry about the crate first. Take my chances with the Todo brothers. If I can get to the crate in time, it might not even matter anyway.

But I feel a bit bored again with the journey. It's been an hour since we met Miss Gia. I turn to her, and she's mumbling to herself. Sometimes she even cackles for no discernable reason to Jake's dismay. It's as if she's lost in her own little world. It took her around half-an-hour to answer me when I asked her for her name.

Is it even her name? Or did she just blurt out "Gia?"

It'd be interesting if I got dementia here. I'd be lost in my own little world, in another world, away from my actual world. I'd be confused shitless.

The thoughts we entertain in boredom. There were deer-like things earlier. Some birds. I try to picture them for little bit. Take in that I'm in another world. But the truth is humans adapt quickly. This just feels like an extension to another space my life takes place in. Something akin to taking a vacation in another country.

I look at Jake. His squinty little face has been frozen in time for a while now. I'm usually good at figuring out people, but I can't even begin to guess what he must be thinking about.

What kind of music does he listen to, I wonder.

Death metal and gangster rap. With occasional Taylor Swift when no one's watching.

The more and more I get to know the kid, the more and more I realize he's the type that just... does things. No, that's putting it too simply. He obviously intellectualizes what he does... there's a compass in there. But all the values are determined solely by him. That's why, I realized, some of his actions don't make sense. It doesn't have to make sense to others.

An entirely selfish being. Self-motivated. Self-guided. To the rest of us, he's a chaos, but in his mind... in his life... in his eyes... he's a steel arrow.

I've met a few like this before. Mostly in law school and law enforcement. Something about the position of power that attracts people like him. I have a hunch the military may be filled with kids like these.

He could use a wake-up call. But I wonder if that'll help him take in the idea that there's a whole world around him with other people that have lives and thoughts just like him, or simply shake the little Yahtzee into something even more indecipherable. Make sense of his wake-up call in his own twisted way.

Oh look, a clearing.

Finally something.

Smoke.

My gut feeling says my luck, or lack of it, followed me all the way here.

"Smoke!" Miss Gia says.

She turns and looks at me.

"Smoooooooke," she repeats.

I smile and nod.

Jake doesn't seem particularly interested in the smoke.

It's a small town. Village is probably a better word for it. Farming village. A lot of fields with some sort of crop. Small houses scattered about accompanying the fields. The land is flat, and from the path we can see the whole thing. Even the field that's the source of the smoke. They managed to put it out, it seems.

An entire year's work literally turned to ash. That's gotta suck.

We make it down to the burnt field and find a group of twenty or so people in a heated discussion. That's probably the entire town we're looking at.

"If we give them what they want, they'll keep coming back. They already took Yori's daughter and Tonn's son, and now we're going to give them our year's work? It's been hard as it is. It's not like we make enough for ourselves these days!" one of them cries out.

"It's the damn king's fault. Can't keep anything in line!" Another one of them yells.

Does the king really matter?

A young teen girl tugs on the sleeve of the man who seems to be in charge of this town. She points at us. The girl looks like a little blond doll. Jake's eyes have been locked in on her since he could see her golden hair glimmering in the sun.

Down, boy. Down.

"Oh, and who the hell are these clowns supposed to be?" the one complaining about the king yells.

The leader of the farmers makes his way towards us. A blonde, bearded man. His body is stout and shows the years of farming work carved onto his body.

His young daughter follows behind him. A middle-age woman, who I guess is his wife, walks next to the daughter.

"Sorry, travelers," he says. "We can't accommodate anyone right now. We can provide some supplies, but we advise you go on your way."

Miss Gia seems to be focused on the young girl as well, but in a more innocent way. Perhaps she reminds her of someone. Or perhaps she just appreciates the girl's beauty as simple beauty without lust. The bird we've been following gently lands on Miss Gia's head.

Interesting. Those birds are commanded by the sorcery that creates them to be attracted to the one wearing the ring: me.

"Roost," I command the bird. It lands on my hand and turns to a small statue again. I place it in the bag Mr. Lor gave me.

"What happened here?" Jake asks. There's sort of a heroic tone to his voice.

"I…" The leader of the farmers clears his throat. "We had a raid by a group of beastmen. Burned our crops. Killed some of the animals. And took…"

He lowers his voice a bit.

"Took some of the children. They demanded that we prepare a payment for them by sunset. Crops, supplies, and equipment. If not, they said they'll simply take them by force and more of our children," the leader of the farmer continues. "Thankfully my wife and daughter were away at the time. But the market being as bad as it is… we won't survive if we give away our crops and supplies… and obviously we can't imagine our children being their slaves. We've sent a few capable men and women to go to the nearest village to report to the magistrate so…"

The leader looks back at his young, worried daughter.

"Why come back?" I ask. "What's the point? Why not stay here and see it through?"

They seem a bit startled at my glacial attitude. I didn't mean to seem uncaring. I just want things to make sense. That's sometimes too much to ask of any world.

"They seemed like they were in a hurry. Had some luggage with them. The cart they had was covered, but from the little we saw they looked like large metal chests," the leader of the farmers answers.

Jake gives me a look.

"Yeah," I answer his look. "But it's doubtful they

have mine. The bird seemed like it was trying to go past this town. I'm guessing the raiders went into the forest."

"They did," the leader answers.

"But you can help us!" the young daughter speaks up. "You all look like seasoned travelers. And you—"

She points to me.

"—Those clothes can't be of this world. You must be an Otherworlder! We've all heard tales of the Otherworlders. How fierce and monstrous they are!"

"Jenna!" The father scolds the daughter.

I'm not sure if she noticed, but Jake's eyes have been glued to her this whole time.

We need to decline. This isn't our problem. The Azure Guards will be here soon enough. The magistrates might make it in time. The beastmen will probably send out some patrol to see if any official forces have arrived and if they see any, they'll flee. Their package is too hot. Maybe I'll come back here and give them some business pointers.

"Sorry—"

"We'll do it," Jake cuts me off.

Really? Really, you horny little psycho? You're going to risk your life to impress a girl who's clearly too young for you to have any good reason to have any temptations for?

"Please." The girl grabs my hand and gives me the puppy dog eyes.

Welcome to the real world, little girl.

We have to learn to not only live on after doing ugly things but also live on after allowing ugly things to happen.

"Hey," Jake sounds gentlemanly as he takes her hand into his.

She's startled and looks a bit afraid that he's holding her hand.

"Leave it to us," he says with a smile.

She's too young, you bastard.

"Wonderful! My name is Vohn. There were three of them here." The father, Vohn, shakes each of our hands.

Jake shakes it confidently.

I shake it begrudgingly.

Miss Gia seems happily confused.

He then waves over other farmers.

"We can tell you guys where they went to, and we'll reward you with whatever we can. If you guys can even distract them until the magistrates arrive, then we should be fine."

I sigh.

No one cares.

I say nothing.

***

All the luggage the bandits were carrying made a hell of a trail. Not too hard to find them from the general direction the farmers gave us. These guys were probably lackeys. Too dumb to have coordinated the robbery. They were probably given better escape directions as well, but they were too dumb to follow them. Causing a backend mess.

"You sure you know how to use that thing?" Jake kicks at the sword we looted from Fuck-Your-Sister that's on my waist now.

"Kind of?" I never used swords much.

"And why is she with us again?" Jake asks as he glances at Miss Gia.

"Because she didn't want to stay there," I answer. Am I hoping too much that her staff has some sort of life saving enchantment?

"No way in hell she's a fighter. I ain't going to put my neck out to save her if she gets herself in trouble," Jake says as if he read my mind.

Shit.

We should have somehow left her back there.

If she gets killed, I'll carry that with me for a while.

"YOU GOT THAT GRANDMA?" Jake yells at Miss Gia. "HIDE OR DIE!"

Miss Gia looks at Jake with disdain.

"She's not deaf, Jake," I tell Jake.

He scoffs.

A pungent aroma in the air.

I see.

We're getting close.

"What's that smell?" Jake asks.

I recognize the smell but don't want to say it.

Soon we come to a clearing.

A woman dressed in fur is dragging a naked young

boy by his hair. He's alive. Barely. Beaten bloody and purple. He's her slave now. Her fuckboy.

But it's the source of the smell that gets my attention.

As she drags him away, she reveals a fire place. The kidnapped daughter is skewered like a pig over the fire. From the look of her, they just setup their dinner. Cut and snapped her jaw so that it'd rest easily over the stick skewering her from her anus to throat. Her limbs tied off to keep her form for easy cooking. Her hair was roughly cut with a knife to keep it short. No one likes the smell of burning hair.

I think she might still be alive.

No. She's not. It's better to believe she's not.

There are two types of beastmen. One is an inexplicable kind of beastmen best described as human... animals. Is humanoid the term? Some of the citizens of this world thought they were gods having fun. Then there are these kinds. Humans who use a type of sorcery to turn into beasts. Funnily enough, it's the latter that has a penchant for eating human flesh. They believed that eating them would make them more primal and distance themselves from their human origin. In short, they eat humans to get stronger. Psychologically, I feel like there's some logic there somewhere.

I made a vow to never do business with their kind of beastmen.

The beastwoman looks at us for a moment. The other two sitting by the fire stand as well. They don't really seem to care.

Cocky.

The woman keeps dragging away the boy who whimpers. Not sure if he can even see us—the rescue—

with his puffed up, beaten eyes.

But I'm still on the skewered girl.

My blood is boiling.

Fuckin' Jake.

I'm invested.

We're all waiting for someone to say something. To start something.

"Yo!" Jake calls out to them.

The two men look at one another. One looks a bit annoyed that he has to be the one to confront us. He sluggishly picks himself up and grabs his brutish looking sword. Probably the one he was going to use to chop off the girl once she was done cooking. They don't have to use such brutish looking swords. They just choose to.

"Your armor," I ask Jake a question I should have asked much earlier. "Is it enchanted?"

If so, we may have a chance. Depending on the quality, the stamp plus his armor should make him pretty damn superhuman.

"Yeah," Jake says. "But I'm not going to use it here. Todo brothers."

"What about the bombs?" I ask.

"Not here," Jake answers quickly. "That's for Redtails."

"Jesus," I say. "Just focus on surviving this first, yeah?"

I turn to Miss Gia. Her eyes are wide but focused. I can't tell what she's thinking. I can't tell if she understands what situation she's in. She's quiet. Gripping her old wooden staff tight.

But I do understand that she didn't understand Jake's instructions earlier.

I give her my bag.

"Your job is to guard this and go find a place to hide." I gently place my hand on Miss Gia's shoulder. I'm not sure if I got through to her.

"Yeah? What do you want?" The beastman finally makes his way over to us.

Jake draws his blade. He doesn't give the guy a verbal answer. He swings and catches the beastman by surprise. The beastmen swings his blade and Jake barely dodges. The beastman can handle himself, but empowered by the stamp, Jake overpowers the bandit pretty handily. The beastman might be more skilled than Jake, but he's not skilled enough to close the supernatural gap.

Not yet at least.

The female runs after Jake with her axe in her hand. I draw my blade.

I intervene and swing hard at her. The swing feels a bit awkward. She dodges easily.

I catch Jake glancing at me. But before he can say anything, he has to dodge a blow from his own opponent.

She's smirking. That bitch. Her shoulders relax and she casually holds… almost dangles the axe by her side.

"Don't swing a sword like a… like a… club!" Jake yells between his blows and dodges.

I know. I know. It's just been a while. You don't really swing swords as a lawyer. Though sometimes that might be nice.

"Damn it!" The bandit cries as Jake kicks him hard in the stomach and pushes him back.

Jake has a smug smile on his face. Don't get cocky, kid. All it takes is a little push in one direction to turn a fight.

The third one in the back is still busy just cooking the poor girl. He's putting some kind of spices on her now.

The beastman finally decides to turn. It's quick. It sounds like his flesh is ripping apart as he explodes into his new shape and size.

A bear? Of Sort? But he has a black mane and bison-like horns. I don't think I've ever seen this kind of creature.

He tosses aside his sword and punches Jake who flies through the air. His armor is glowing with deep crimson symbols.

It seems Jake changed his mind about not using his armor. He'll be fine.

How about me though?

I look at the beastwoman, and she doesn't hesitate to turn herself. She looks like a wolf of sort. A dog. A bitch. Fitting.

Bitch.

She doesn't toss her weapon. In fact, she's licking it. This shit's getting ridiculous.

These guys didn't need any instruments or incantations to turn. They're dumb, but they're experienced. Skilled. Expected of the ones hired for robbing a branch of the banking guild.

We were a bit naïve about this whole thing.

No backing out now.

Risk death over dying.

I look back to check on Miss Gia. She's staring

intently at something, but I'm not really sure what.

The bitch's faster than I thought. By the time I turned my head, she was on me.

Shit.

I hear Miss Gia's war cry.

She throws my bag at the Bitch.

The Bitch grabs the bag and throws it onto the ground. Then stomps it a few times.

There goes the bird.

Miss Gia looks absolutely surprised at this turn of events.

Another war cry from the old woman.

She swings her walking stick at the Bitch.

The Bitch deflects it easily and knocks Miss Gia onto her ass. The stick is shattered. It's just a stick.

Miss Gia looks flabbergasted.

The Bitch looks at Miss Gia for a moment, but rightfully determines the old woman will play no significant role in this fight.

But I don't take the chance for her to change her mind and thrust my sword at her.

It barely breaks through her fur and skin. I retract the sword quick and see a little bit of blood on the tip.

I look back at Jake. He's stabbing his sword through his opponent's heart. There's a giddy smile on his face. He's feeling it. Getting stronger. The full stamp gives us more strength the more we kill. It's euphoric when you feel it. The energy that courses through your veins. Your mind gets brighter.

Not to mention there's just something gratifying to our primal core of taking someone else's life. All the stories they told and had to tell. Gone. By our hands.

Killing can be addictive. Especially for Otherworlders in this world.

The Bitch howls. Her pride's hurt more than anything. The cook finally picks up his own sword. Jake will have to handle him.

I try to imagine the time I killed before. Did I make the same face as Jake?

My trip down memory lane gives me strength. I yearn to fill my stamp. I yearn to get stronger. I have a desperate need for it.

Bring it on, Bitch.

She seems a bit nervous about this new look I have in my eyes.

I leap at her with my sword. My swing still heavy as if I'm swinging down a bat. It's wrong. But it'll do the job.

Nope.

The Bitch smacks it away, and the sword flies out of my hand.

Shit.

Shit. Shit. Shit.

Do I have to resort to that?

Damn it.

"What is now cannot be without what was before…" I incant as I desperately leap around to dodge her swings. Where the fuck is Jake? He's watching the third one flee.

"….Follow the thread connecting the moments that once were and that will be…" Jake's looking at me now. He looks to be in disbelief. A disgusted disbelief. He's slowly making his way towards me.

"…Fickle but determined patroness of moments, Oslo. Manifest." Disgusted that I can cast a spell. I finish my incantation. Just in time.

I can't dodge the last blow. The Bitch's axe digs its way through my clavicle and into my lungs and heart.

Radius of 1 meter.

"Shift," I command as blood fills my mouth.

Turn back 3 seconds.

Her axe buried deep into my chest lifts away and my flesh closes back.

Unfortunately, I feel everything.

The stamp drains out to an outline to simply keep me alive. Not from the wound. But from the spell. Though the wound probably didn't help.

I feel dizzy.

I need to kill something.

Nausea.

I NEED to kill something.

Recover.

Hold on, you weakass bastard.

Pussy.

Don't die like this.

If you die, you die. But don't die without trying.

Go kill something.

I tumble towards my sword and grip it as tight as I can.

The Bitch's arm is back up in the air—to the point before she swung down. She looks confused.

My chance.

I swing hard. Pushing the sword down as hard as I can. Right down her shoulder. It gets stuck.

Blood spurts.

She howls.

That was everything that I had. But it's not enough.

Her axe is about to swing down again.

"I said don't swing a sword like a club!" Jake yells. Bastard finally helps.

Jake pierces the bitch's throat and she goes down.

I fall to my knee and drop the sword to the ground. The sun feels hot. I'm sweating.

It wasn't my kill.

Fuck.

"You can use magic?!" Jake asks. He sounds as if he's so envious that he's disgusted. As if someone like me could use it but he can't.

Violent coughs are one of the things I hate the most about being alive. But I can't stop coughing.

"Hey!" Jake shakes me.

Fuck off, kid.

"Yo! You know how to use magic?!" He sounds annoyed. "The fuck, man?! Yo! Answer me!"

"It's not exactly what you think," I tell him to get him off my case. Wonder if he just saved me to ask me about the magic.

The third one. Where did he flee to?

We can still smell his roast.

How were they planning to take the farmers' annual worth of work and their equipment?

I see more of them behind Jake.

Right.

"Shit," my remark turns Jake's head.

"Fuck you and your fucking luck, man," Jake complains.

A band of ten of them. Maybe twelve. The number doesn't really matter. We can't handle this. Not with his skills. Not with my state.

We're fucked.

They march confidently towards us. Each step growing stronger with anger. With hatred.

"You want to die with us, grandma?" Jake asks.

Miss Gia. She's standing right behind us. I didn't even hear her coming.

She's quiet. I think her lips are moving. I'm not sure.

The sky turns ashen, and it begins to pour rain.

Each raindrop glistens rainbow like oil. It pours everywhere except around the three of us.

The beastmen are startled for a moment but realize the rainbow raindrops seem harmless.

I'm not so sure. My instincts say otherwise.

They come for us again.

"Rain?! That's the magic you decide to use at this moment?!" Jake readies his sword. Before he lunges, I put my arm out in wait. "Damn it, this fuckin' retarded grandma!"

"Wait," I warn him.

One of the beastmen begins to cry. She's in hysteria. She's staring at her hands that's melting off as each drop of the rain turns her flesh, bone, and all into water. She's pooling beneath her feet and there will be nothing of her left as she seeps into the earth.

All the other beastmen begin to panic as they notice the same effect on themselves. A few begin charging our way. One falls as his leg loses enough flesh and muscle. Even his bone is turning liquid. Into water.

The old woman swipes her finger left to right and then up and down.

A gentle, translucent white light forms a thin wall in

front of us.

The old woman gently flicks all her fingers in front of her and mouths a word in silence and with a smile.

The wall begins to move forward and push back the beastmen. They seem helpless as they melt away.

The rain stops.

Clouds dissipates like an illusion.

It's the orange sky again.

The only signs of the band of beastmen are puddles and scraps of drenched attire.

Neither Jake nor I understood exactly what we witnessed. But even we knew her incantation was too quick for the grand spectacle she had showed. What we saw was something masterful.

The legend is still within you, Miss Gia. We can run from the past. Get as far away from it as possible. Sometimes by choice, sometimes by fate. But we can't erase it.

I look at her. She looks at me with giddy eyes and the smile of a child. She seems proud of what she's done. The slaughter. The power. Or maybe she feels happy that she was able to relive her youth a bit for the moment. The vitality that comes with youth.

I say nothing.

I return a smile. It feels weird because I still don't know if I condone how proud and genuinely happy she is. I feel parental towards her even though I have no right to.

We head back.

Jake says nothing the entire way. He looks disgruntled. His moment of victory cockblocked by a businessman and a homeless elderly woman both using sorcery beyond anything he could have imagined.

She shut him up.

Good.

***

We return. Our survival tells the farmers that our mission was a success.

The welcome to our news is lukewarm. It's understandable. An awkward sense of joy. Celebrated not by cheers and clapping, but by screaming, sobbing mothers who just lost their children.

The leader of the farmers—I think Vohn is the name—guides us to his home. His daughter follows closely behind him. She's looking at us with admiration. Even the grumpy Jake who's still butt-hurt about the sorcery thing. But she's a smart girl. She knows not to feel joyous about her heroes return. She knows that the day was about survival and lucky survivors. It was a day for mourning and respect rather than celebration.

But at his home, private from the rest of the town, Vohn and his family treat us to a feast.

Miss Gia seems to be really happy with the festivities. There's a smile on her face, and that's more than enough out of her to know that she's genuinely happy where she is. Her eyes are glowing.

A lot of laughter, a lot of drinking, and everything becomes a bit of a blur.

"Yo. How did you learn to do magic?"

"It's complicated," I tell him.

"Seriously, where did you learn it?"

"Let it go," I tell him.

"I even sought out wizards and, like, their little academy to see if I could learn, man."

"Sorry." Not really. Why should I be?

"Do you know how fucking lucky you are?"

"Get over it. It's like anything else in life. Some of us just get things others don't." I finally lost my patience. I don't know why I was so patient with him in the first place. Maybe because I do realize how lucky it was for me to even have that spell.

But at the same time, it's not like it didn't come with a price. Complaining about having a good thing that you didn't ask for is a dick move. But complaining about having to pay a price for something you didn't ask for is just being a reasonable human.

But I enjoy the rest of the party. If I'm honest with myself, I feel as if I earned this small celebration. A small moment in time where I can lose myself to some joy despite what I still had to accomplish.

She's not getting any less pregnant.

That Redtails is still out there.

My crate is in the hands of some frog assholes.

I ruined my own fun.

I fell asleep at some point, but wake up to bed squeaks from next door. I must have woken up to the end of it. There's an almost haunting silence as I realize the room next to ours is the farmer's young daughter's. Then I hear her crying.

I pick myself up from the bed and see Miss Gia sitting by the small table in the room. The second bed in the room that was for Miss Gia is empty. I was hoping I'd see Jake there. Her eyes are wide open. She's muttering something to herself. Her eyes turn toward me.

"I watched him go," she says. "He watched me watching him go. I let him go."

"I listened," she continues. "She didn't say yes."

Shit.

"But she didn't say no." She sounds confounded. "Why do I feel like I did something wrong?"

I can piece together how it might have gone.

Jake goes into her room.

Drunk. The nauseating aroma of wine still sweating out from his pores.

She's confused. Young and not even in the right world to know what to expect from something like this.

He coerces her softly and gently.

Mentions something about how he's a hero. He saved their lives. They owe them one.

And then it just takes the smallest push. A small amount of force on his part to let her know who's in control and who's not.

Then the tumble begins.

The momentum takes over.

Innocence is lost somewhere along the line.

She's spilling worthless tears.

He'll forget her by the next time he finds his next thing to stick his dick into.

She'll remember this longer than she wants to.

He's probably sleeping. Satiated and proud.

She's too young, Jake.

But to you, it doesn't matter, right?

It's not our world. Not our rules. Not our laws.

She's looking at me as if it was rape. Or if it's okay. She wants me to tell her it's okay. It's just sex. It's nothing. No need to feel bad about it. No need for us to care about it.

I say nothing.

I simply hold her hand and sit next to her.

It is rape.

I'd consider it rape.

Not just statutory, but just rape.

But I say nothing.

Maybe I'm over-romanticizing and over-thinking everything. People are allowed to fuck.

No reason to upset her further.

The door opens. Jake stumbles in still drunk from sex and wine.

He sees us sitting by the coffee table. Our judging eyes.

Now he feels a bit uncomfortable.

But he ignores us and collapses on the bed.

Sometime afterwards, I fall asleep sitting by the table.

***

I wake up to a snoring Jake. Miss Gia is gone. Beneath my hand is the small medallion I refused earlier. I feel even less deserving of it now than I did before.

Jake eventually wakes up. I could have woken him up earlier, but I feel disgusted.

He looks at me like he's offended that I'm judging him.

"You're a real piece of shit, Jake," I say, breaking the silence.

"Fuck you too, man," Jake replies accordingly.

He doesn't ask about Miss Gia. He's probably just glad.

We gather our things and head downstairs. It's Vohn who sees us first. He looks… bitter and melancholy. The mom quietly removes herself from the room.

"I packed you two some bread and milk for your breakfast," he says, indicating the basket on the table.

"Awesome." Jake hurries for the basket.

No breakfast with the family. They just want us to leave. Understandable. I feel guilty, but can't really find the words to say anything.

Say something.

But what's there to say?

Say nothing.

We get back on the road.

"What now then?" Jake asks. "You lost the bird, right?"

"Straight down that path is the mountains. It's

closer than going back to Mardosa. I figured I might as well check," I tell him. "Turn back to grab another bird if nothing's there."

"Am I still getting paid if I come?" Jake asks.

I ponder for a moment. My stamp is slightly refilled, but still less than when I started.

"Yeah," I answer.

Jake and I don't talk after that.

Silence is nice.

Do I have any right to judge this kid?

We've all done shit before.

I wonder how many girls I messed up with their perspective on men and human relationships?

But do gamblers have no right to tell others to not gamble? Couldn't one say they're the ones who know better than anyone else what gambling can do?

And why is it that the older we get, the less we appreciate people who simply do whatever they want to get whatever they want, and yet somewhere deep inside, we admire them at the same time.

Not that I wanted to sleep with that girl.

But just the audacity of it.

Or is it just me?

Maybe it's just me.

"Who the fuck are you to judge, anyways?" Jake says. "Baby-mama-ditchin'-bastard."

We're in mountain ridges by the time he spoke.

I don't give him a response. Fuck you, Jake. I've been trying to figure that out myself. Who am I not to judge?

Fuck it. I'll judge you. You judge me. That's what our brains are for.

The path is coarse and rugged. It hasn't been travelled for a while. If the Todo brothers used a cart to carry the crates, they also made sure to at least cover up the tracks they left.

How do we find these guys?

Then I hear it. The heavy footsteps. Something's coming our way.

Jake and I only need to share a quick glance before we decide to hide in the bushes.

It's a giant, toad-like, thing. It looks even bigger than I remember. Wider and more muscular too. He carries with him a club that's the size of a small tree. It's one of the Todo brothers.

He doesn't look happy. Grumbling to himself something. Ribbiting once in a while. An angry ribbit.

The toad stops right in front of us.

Fuck.

Jake seems to be thinking the same.

He pulls aside his loincloth and whips out his giant penis.

We're going to get pissed on.

Jake looks horrified.

He turns the other way and pisses there instead.

Thank. God.

We can see the steam of his piss from all the way here. The air is filled with a salty and pungent stench.

He lets out a satisfied ribbit before going down the

path we came.

"So they're here," I whisper to Jake.

"And how are we going to fight them?" Jake asks.

"I just need to get to the crate. Maybe we can sneak by," I tell Jake.

"The other brother is probably guarding them! Dumbass!" Jake snaps.

"Remember the poison bomb you mentioned before? The one to kill Redtails?"

"Yeah, we're not using them here."

"How potent are they?"

"Potent enough to bring down one of them dinosaur-sized looking things. That's what they were made for."

"I'll pay for them."

Jake seems to be calculating.

"Fine," Jake says. "That's not coming out of my payment."

"Of course not." I offer my hand.

We shake on it.

The big toad left prints on the path. Being giant has its downsides. So does being whatever he is. There's a sulfuric musk in the air. We follow both up the path for a while until it veers off into the woods. Then we follow the smell and broken leaves and branches off into the heavy greens.

That takes off some guess work, but we come to a cliff edge. Below is a cave and there's a cart parked outside. More importantly, the other giant toad-man is there, and he's carrying a club as big as his brother's.

"Look," Jake says, pointing at the cave. The crates are visible. An assortment blue and black.

"Alright. Throw the bomb," I tell Jake.

"What if I miss?"

"Don't miss then."

"No, we'll do it up close and personal. It'll kill him anyways." From one of the pouches strapped around his waist, Jake pulls out a small racquetball sized glass ball. It's filled with a greyish liquid and some sparkling dust.

That's when I got the gut wrenching feeling that this wasn't going to work.

Looks more like some kind of makeup than a poison bomb.

We slide down the cliff, and it gets the toad's attention right away.

He roars. Sounds like a mad bull.

The toad swings his club right around where we'd land, and we both leap out of the way. I draw my sword. I'm sure I'll be useless. I should just run for the crates.

Jakes leaps out of the way and throws his glass ball.

It hits the toad solidly on his head and explodes into dark gray smoke.

"Shit!" I yell as I run out of the way.

The smoke forms into a giant sphere and stays there. I guess there's magic involved to contain it to kill just what it needs to kill.

Jake comes beside me.

"Got that bitch," he says with a smirk.

"You could have killed me, you bastard," I tell him.

He shrugs.

Another bull-like roar.

The giant toad soars out of the smoke dome and swings down his club at Jake. It misses his head by a hair and tears through his armor instead. The force knocks Jake on his ass.

"Shit!" I yell as I grab Jake by his wrist and drag him away as far as I can. Jake's squinty eyes are as wide as they can be. He cheated death.

The toad is coughing, but he seems mostly fine. Maybe whatever he is makes him immune to the poisons that are supposed to take down 'dinosaurs.' Or maybe the poison was garbage. Doesn't really matter either way at this point.

"So what now?!" Jake picks himself up and asks. He draws his sword.

I shake my head. I have no idea. I look at the caves again. I can just run for it.

Jake loudly 'tsk's.

"You got magic, don't ya?" He asks with unconcealed jealousy.

"It's not what you think," I tell him. "And I'd need some serious back-up energy to survive using it."

"That's a pretty useless spell then." Jake seems to find some joy in my limitations.

The toad roars and huffs.

"I'll chew on your heads alive," the toad speaks. His voice like charcoal scraping against brick is far more menacing than I'd like to admit.

"Oh shit," Jake says. But he's not looking at the toad.

He's looking up at the ledge above all of us.

I look up. A figure in black armor with long red lashes for the plume of his helm is looking down at us.

Redtails.

He disappears into puff of smoke and reappears in the cave by the crates.

The Todo brother looks lost.

Redtails has a crest. He's searching for his crate.

A black crate. That's the crate he's looking for.

Redtails has no concern for our fight.

He places a parchment over the crate and draws a symbol on it. The crate glows for a moment and then disappears.

"Hey," the toad growls.

Redtails nods at the toad and walks off.

He's saying we can continue doing what we were doing now.

The angry toad swings his giant club at Redtails.

Redtails disappears and reappears above the toad. In his hand, a spear with a golden blade. As soon as he stabs the toad, a flash of light and a crack of lightning strikes through the beastman and tears him in two. Not a clean bisection. His blood and guts splatter all over.

Redtails disappears into a puff of smoke again, landing away from the mess. His spear vanishes into smoke from his hand.

"S-shit!" Jake's stunned.

Redtails is staring at me. Or at least looking at my

direction. I stare back.

He seems to suddenly lose interest and walks past us. He disappears into a puff of smoke again.

We hear a stampede of footsteps coming from below. The other brother is on his way.

"I guess he heard all that." Jake's nerves seem to be getting the better of him. He seems off his edge.

I run for the crates. There can only be so many blue crates and black crates in the first place. It doesn't take me long to find mine with the crest.

I open it up. It's not much, but it's all there. The money. The stuff. Most importantly, my helm.

"Damn that Redtails," Jake swears. He's looking over my shoulder. He wants to just grab the money and run.

"He's not Redtails," I correct Jake.

Put on the helm.

Come back home.

As soon as I set the helm on my head, the rest of the armor appears over my body like a smoky apparition. It solidifies. I am home.

From the tip of the helm, lashes of red light stretch out like whips and forms the "red tails."

I grip the dark steel club. It doesn't feel unfamiliar. It doesn't feel as if any time has passed since I gripped it last.

My hand feels home.

The toad roars at the sight of his massacred brother's body.

Sounds like a cannon-sized bullhorn.

I leap, turn into smoke, and disappear from sight.

In an instant I form from smoke again, and I'm above the other Todo brother. The speed will take getting used to again.

I swing my metal club. The blow obliterates the amphibian giant's skull, and it erupts in blood and guts. In some sick sense, the eyeballs bursting out amuses me.

I ride the giant's body as it drops to the ground.

Euphoria. I feel my stamp filling up. It's still not one hundred percent. A Todo brother isn't enough. Not for me anyways.

Jake looks disgruntled.

"You were Redtails this whole time, you asshole?" Jake asks.

I get off the dead frogman and approach Jake. His hand holding the sword twitches a bit, but he doesn't ready it.

Is it out of friendship or fear, I wonder.

"Then who's that other guy?" he asks before I even have the time to answer.

"I don't know." I really don't. "I'm going to find out."

Jake doesn't seem really sure what to do or say. He's just looking disgruntled.

"Well?" I want to give him a shot. A bit childish of me, really. I simply want to see if he even wants to try. "Do you still want to kill Redtails?"

He doesn't say either yes or no. Doesn't even show any body movement.

"You can do a lot of good for the people here, Jake." Why am I preaching to him? "You can do a lot of wrong as well. That's the same either here or back home."

He's curious where I'm going with this. Where am I going with this?

"Do something more with your life than just getting what you want." I dissipate my dark club. It'll come when I need it again.

I turn my back to him.

"You think I'm a motherfucking joke?"

I don't see it, but I hear it. The flames igniting and his scream. I'm sure he tried to grab the lashes.

I spin around and see in his hand another one of his poison bombs. His other hand he's staring at it in pain. It's burnt. It'll heal. He has his stamp.

Don't throw the bomb, Jake. Be smart.

He throws the bomb.

I appear beside him with my club already swinging at the side of his head.

He drops to the ground. His left eye popped out somewhere along with a chunk of his face and skull.

What do I do with this guy?

He'll lose the eye, but he'll live. It'll probably end up eating up most of his stamp.

"My eye," He moans. "Use your magic."

He's pleading.

He's moaning.

Almost sounds like he's crying.

I take my helm off briefly to put on my earphones again.

I turn it on and rewind.

"No," I tell him.

Do I kill him? But why did I leave here in the first place? What were the consequences of being judge, jury, and executioner when the lawyer left the room?

I won't kill him.

Take it as a life lesson. Lesson of humility. An eye is a small price.

I'll drop him off at the nearest town that's not the farm. Then I have a faker to chase.

Then again.

Why did I start killing in the first place?

I start the music around where I left off before. I hum it as I carry Jake over my shoulder.

"Emptiness, a lonely parody. And my life, another smokin' gun a sign of my indifference."

Episode 3 ✋ Tay's Crate

Episode 4

Bob and Robert

Nasha.

My goddess. My angel. My principle.

Who would have thought when I stumbled onto this world that I'd discover the life that was always meant for me. Each morning, I wake up to her baking bread and cooking soup. No dream could compare to the sight of her when I open my eyes. It's always the same. A soft smile on her face as she stirs the pot over the hearth. She hums a gentle tune. Always the same. But never enough.

"Good morning." I always greet her first. And every morning when I do, she spins her head towards me.

She breaks into a wide smile, walks on over, and gives me a kiss on my forehead before whispering, "Morning."

I'm not a man who deserve this. Mid-40s. Receding hairline. Body carrying the weight of an old man's appetite with none of the young man's metabolism.

Don't think about it, Robert.

Can't change age.

Besides, you ain't no weak pussy. The muscles are there. It's just blurred and buried. And here? In this world? You're a warrior—a destroyer. This home, as humble as it is, you bought with the money you've earned slaying beasts, creatures, and assholes that people feared. Feared for good reasons. But you did it. You were the one who taught them that the world is a big place and they were just another tiny part of it.

Besides, this humble home's still one of the bigger ones in the town. We had to get the one with two bedrooms. One for the boy. The other for guests that may come by. And the living room is our domain. Kind of odd. Apparently a remnant from how their homes used to be in ancient times. When in Rome, as they say.

That woman—your queen—chose you to be her guardian. You've earned it. And soon, you'll be her king.

Shit.

I still don't deserve her. But I should always feel that way. Never take her for granted.

"Morning, Robert," she says it the second time as she usually does, but with my name. The insignia's translation is funny with stuff like names. I hear the name as she tries to pronounce it in her tongue unlike other words that I simply hear in my head with their translations. Her 'Robert' sounds more like 'Ro-bhart' with a gentle emphasis on the ending 't'.

Before the boy wakes up—which will be sooner than later—I pull my woman into me. She giggles. My siren. I'm feeling playful today. We kiss passionately as her arms find their way to wrap around me. Her right hand caresses my shoulder as her left gently brushes through my hair. Her eyes are closed and her tongue dances with mine.

We pause for a moment. She giggles again. I wonder if we have more time.

"Torin will be up soon," she warns. Torin. My wonderful boy of five. Named after the grandfather of his father who passed away. I admit it makes me a bit more comfortable that it was the grandfather and not the father.

"We can go hide in the guest room," I suggest.

She guffaws and playfully slaps my arm.

"Come have breakfast." She frees herself from me and heads for the soup again. The bread is already on the table.

I was only half kidding.

The door to the boy's room creaks open.

"Can I come out now?" The boy asks carefully.

My angel blushes red and smiles.

"You can come out anytime you want, champ!" My words reach the boy quick, and he darts out from the room and jumps on top of me. I pick him up and gently toss him onto bed. He laughs. I laugh.

Nasha starts ringing the small bell above the hearth, signifying the meal is ready.

"No more of that." She's already setting the last bowl of soup onto the table. "It's time to eat."

We listen like good soldiers. Nasha is a bit strict with the table etiquette. I like that. It shows strength.

"Sometimes I'm afraid that you won't come back," she says as she tears the large bread into chunks and puts it on each of our plates. I get the first share. Then her. Then the boy.

"I'll always come back." I dunk the bread into the soup. Nasha first found that to be very crude but soon learned to make an exception for this little antic I brought from my world. She does it as well now. I'm rubbing off on her.

"I wanted to surprise you, but this time I thought maybe I'll move here for good," I tell her.

Her eyes glow and face brightens up. But before she can express her joy, the boy screams in happiness and runs over to me and gives me a hug.

"Are you serious? Do you truly mean that?" Nasha eyes are tearing up. "I should tell our friends and we can have a little celebration."

"Little? We'll do a big celebration. A feast!" I can't

understand what I'm feeling now. But it's powerful… and good. Like a drug. I'm not sure if I ever felt this happy before. To feel this wanted. I just have to make sure I do what I must to take care of my life back home so that I can be here in good conscience.

"Thank you," I tell them. My own eyes are watering up now.

Nasha looks happily confused.

"For what?" She asks as she finally lets the tears drop as well. She smiles and chuckles.

I don't answer. I hope they just know. I give the boy a kiss on his forehead and we finish our breakfast.

***

I pack light. Just need some water and a snack to make it to the mountains. The exit is somewhere halfway up the mountain and off the side of the beaten path. When I first came through that waypoint, I thought I was going to die lost in the mountains. Conqueror of beasts and bandits killed by the wilderness. So I pack light, but I pack smart. Have all my necessities. Not going to lose my family or have them lose me over carelessness or cockiness.

Nasha hands me my snack. A wrap of sorts.

"I'll be back by tomorrow," I assure her and give her a kiss.

"I'll be waiting," she tells me.

I wave them good bye. It's still morning when I leave. The town is bustling with people starting their days. Many know me here. I'm well-liked. It takes a bit of time getting out of town as I get through all the people greeting me and wanting small talk.

It takes another hour to reach the mountains. A distance that'd normally take most people about two hours. The insignia and its perks.

From there, about half-an-hour to get to the point of the path that I need to veer off from. That point is easy to remember. Can't miss it. It's at a point where you can see the entire town. I can see my house from here. Nasha is probably preparing lunch for Torin by now. I'll be back soon.

From here on, it's about fifteen minutes out into the woods. And soon, I stand beneath familiar green trees and in the middle of a somewhat familiar jungle of greens.

I look at my insignia. It's full. As always.

"Let me out," I ask the old man. I'm glad there are no magic words for me to remember. Just need to know where the exit points are and have a full insignia to talk to him and to leave. I was told there are other ways to leave this world, but the old man doesn't recommend them.

You ready to go?

I hear his voice in my head.

"Yep," I tell him.

A crack of light opens in front of me. As I take a step into it, I feel my body dissipate.

When I come to, I'm in the darkness. Just need to walk for a bit until I see the door. It's a weird feeling each time going back and forth. It reminds me of blacking out. But without the pain or dizziness. Just the blank moment.

I think I figured it being about 30 minutes or so of walking last time. Watches don't work in here. They work over there but not in here. Not in the darkness.

Wonder why.

Maybe it's like one of those different dimension things.

Who gives a shit, I suppose.

I see the door.

I knock.

Always takes three knocks.

Hurry up, you bastard.

I miss my family already.

He opens the door.

"Welcome back," the old man says.

"Thanks," I say.

He opens the drawer in his desk and hands me my keys, phone, and wallet.

"Thanks," I tell him again. I check my phone. He kept it charging for me. I check the date. It's been about 4 days since I've left.

As usual, he doesn't ask how it was over there or anything. But he does asks, as usual, "Coming back again?"

"Yeah," I answer. "Soon probably."

"Good." He smiles.

He's a creepy motherfucker.

I nod and leave his little closet.

On the other side of the closet is a 24-hour gas station with a convenience store. No one seems to work here. I ended up checking the back trying to get someone.

I see my car in the parking lot where I left it. It's

night. Not too late. It's raining here. Everything already feels miserable. I miss home.

When I open the car door, the familiar smell of my ride overwhelms my senses. I'm back. It's like time hasn't passed. But I was there in the Otherworld for seven days. It's been four days here. Always got to wrap my head around it. Always trips me up. The time that passes here is never more than how many days have passed on the other side. Once I spent three days there and came back to find that only an hour had passed.

That almost caused problems.

The drive to my house feels long and dreary, and the route feels too familiar. I'm in a whole new world of concrete paved roads for fast moving metal machines, but just the motions of getting around the place feel instinctive. The same streets. Same lights. Same turns. Before I realize it, I'm on auto pilot.

The neighborhood is quiet even though it's not that deep into the night. It's almost unnerving. I pull up to the driveway. Right next to her car. She sees me from the kitchen window and happily waves.

I don't even need to open the door. By the time I get there, she has it open and waiting for me. She pulls me in for a deep hug and kisses me on the cheek.

"Welcome home," she says gently. "You're earlier than you said you'd be."

I usually say I'm gone for the max duration of the time I'm planning to stay in the Otherworld for. Solves a lot of problems with the time inaccuracies.

"Maybe it's fate," she continues as she grabs my hand and guides me through our house to the dining table. "I did make your favorite—Lasagna—for dinner tonight."

It smells wonderful. She's a great cook.

The kids run down. My oldest, fourteen, and my youngest, eight. They give me casual greetings and sit down at the dinner table. It's as if I was never gone for them. Wonder how Torin is doing.

I feel like I'm on auto pilot again. The same faces. Same routines. Same rituals.

It's the bit of chaos that I'm not used to. Kids talking. Eating. Passing around food. They eat so quickly, and before I know it, they're asking if they can be excused. Up to their rooms. To do whatever it is they do. Usually the wife would say no, but this time she allows it. She says she wants to spend some time with me.

"How was your trip?" she asks me as if she cares. It's all just formalities. She comes around and wraps herself around me. Again, just formalities. She goes and grabs the wine for us.

"I missed you," she says. "You know, I ran into Maggie from when I used to work at the mall? You remember her?"

I look at her with a dumb look on my face. My fork poking through the cheese, pasta layer, and the tomato sauce. Over and over. I wait for her to continue her story regardless of my lack of knowledge.

"She has another man already!"

When did she lose the other one, and why am I supposed to give a fuck that she has another one within whatever time frame she lost the other one?

"Anyways, I saw them walking through the grocery store... y'know just going through the produce. Like, they didn't really have anything planned and were just making the dinner recipes then and there..."

145

It's okay if I eat, right? That's not being "inattentive"? I take the risk of putting the lasagna into my mouth as I gauge her reaction.

"…and I don't know. Y'know? It's the little things. It made me really miss you. Kind of… made me mad actually. I guess it's all beautiful in the beginning." She chuckles as she sets my glass of wine by my plate. "I was just jealous. It's been a while since we did something like that."

The little things. I take a sip of my wine.

What happened to me talking about my trip?

"You okay?" she asks. "Did something happen at the trip?"

I look at her dumbly again.

"Yeah. Yeah, yeah," I answer. Before she can ask for more of a story, I put some more lasagna in my mouth. Fill it up. It is delicious to her credit.

She doesn't seem happy by my answer. Not satisfied. But she continues her meal.

"You want seconds?" she asks.

I nod my head.

She finishes her glass of wine before getting up to grab another slice of the lasagna from the tray. After handing me my seconds, she pours herself a second glass of wine.

What's with her?

Maybe I should have a few more glasses of wine. It'll make the rest of the night easier.

We finish dinner mostly in silence. Then we do the dishes together like we always did before we even got married. I did the washing and she did the drying. She didn't like her fingers getting pruney. Usually we turned on our old cassette player as we did them. The player we had since our days in college. I thought, from the mood of the evening, she wouldn't turn it on tonight. But she does. She has a small smile on her face. Other than the music, we wash the dishes in silence.

After doing the dishes, I take a shower and go see the kids to tell them good night.

When I come back to the bedroom, I see her looking through her memory box. The box where she kept the 'souvenirs of our lives' as she called it. Some of the stuff in there went back all the way to the days before we even started dating. Of course she'd do that today.

"Are you leaving me, Bob?" She quietly asks.

I hate that she calls me Bob. It never bothered me before, but Robert... Robert has such a better, stronger sound.

"How'd you know?" I ask more squeamishly than I intended.

But more than that. I hate that I feel nothing now. Home doesn't feel like home. Someone I said I loved feels more distant than a stranger. At least a stranger wouldn't make me feel this awkwardly... oddly... some sort of discomfort. There's a vacuum between us. No, a chasm. Where everything we once were and everything we wanted to be is being sucked into an abyssal void. I sit next to her and it feels uncomfortable to even breathe. The scent of vanilla from her skin smells and feels chemical now.

Everything we've done feels like it was a waste of time or just stepping stones for me to meet Nasha.

But I don't feel sorry at all. We're all responsible for our happiness after all. This not feeling sorry is actually the furnace burning for the courage to do what I must.

"Women know these things," she says. "Hell, I'm sure anyone would have figured it out by now."

She smiles.

"It was a bit obvious, Bob. An affair was the only logical explanation."

I kind of feel offended that what I have with her is reduced to something like an "affair."

"Yeah," I say. Her smile soothes me. I wonder why.

"Well…" She pauses for a moment. "I want… I want to be amicable about this. I know there's no use chasing after someone whose mind's already made up."

"…Thanks." I'm not sure why I said that.

"Thanks?" She makes an odd face. The smile's still there, but it's not the same. It seems that what I said is hard for her to accept. Trying her best to swallow it.

"I'll leave tonight," I tell her.

"You're a father, Bob. You can choose not to be my husband, but you can't stop being a father to our children."

I nod. I think it may have been begrudging nod. I didn't it mean it that way. She saw it that way.

"I'll leave tomorrow then. I'll see them off to school."

"And then?"

"I'll come visit. We'll work it out."

She looks at me without words. I wonder if she's thinking of the money problem. I suppose I can't really tell her the truth.

I'm cutting off ties. Not just with her. But with this

world. She's a good woman. Capable. My kids are smart and strong kids. They'll survive. It'll be just as if I'm dead.

The gentle smile on her face crumbles and her lips begin to twitch. Her eyes water and the thickest tear drops I've ever seen from a person drips down.

"Does that whore at least know?"

Whore?

My mind fills with Nasha's face. She's smiling.

A whore?

"That you're a husband and a father? Does that whore know that she's destroyed our lives?"

She's staring at me if as if I'd...

I can't shake off the face of Nasha.

"...she's not a whore," I mutter.

"What?" She asks in disbelief.

"Nasha's not a whore," I speak more confidently. I'm defending my woman's honor.

"Is that all you can think of right now? In front of me? The woman you married?"

I stare right into her eyes. I won't turn away.

"Bob, you're a piece of shit. I can't believe... all that time... Bob, you're a piece of shit."

That's fine. I deserve that. I'm going to walk away. Go sleep on the couch. Maybe grab a beer from the fridge.

"Go to your whore tonight, Bob. The kids don't nee—"

"SHE'S NOT A WHORE!"

"A WHORE! SHE'S A WHORE! A SLUT! AND I

HOPE THE TWO OF YOU BURN!"

I'm already on top of her. I think I may have struck her twice before I was even in this position. It all happened so fast.

My hands grip around her throat tightly. So tight that I'm surprised my fingers aren't just ripping through the flesh and meeting in the middle. She's flailing. Scratching. Trying to say something.

Why can't I stop?

Tears are pouring from her eyes. Still looking at me. Trying to see something within me that's already long gone for her. Something she saw before.

Stop.

But all I can see is beautiful Nasha. My Nasha smiling. She's probably getting ready for bed right now. Maybe sitting outside looking at the stars. I always tell her not to. She'd catch a cold. What time is it there?

Stop before it's too late.

But there's already only silence.

As if the life of the room faded away with her.

She's stopped flailing. Her eyes are bloodshot and stretched wide staring at the ceiling.

My fingers are still gripping her throat. They remain there, mustering all the strength they have left, to make sure she's gone. Then they remain there in disbelief. How did it go from a quiet conversation to... this? From my wife to a corpse?

I release her, but it's not like she'd mind either way anymore.

My fingers hurt.

I walk into the bathroom and run them under the cold water. I'm not sure why I thought that'd help, but it does. I use the soap to wash my hands. Not sure why I did that either.

I walk out of my room and looked down the hallway. The door straight ahead is the door to my younger son. He's probably asleep now. The door adjacent is my older daughter. She's finally gotten a room of her own. Used to be my office. She's might be asleep or quietly awake and doing things on her phone.

I won't leave my children to be orphans.

I won't.

***

"You look happier than usual to be back today," the man says.

"I think I can finally immigrate for good now," I tell him. By the time I pulled off to the parking lot, I already felt as if I said my goodbyes to this world.

I don't know why, but I take the ring out from my pocket. I guess I'm ready to show off to the whole world. But I have to be careful. I don't want to wear out the moment by showing it off to everyone before the person it's actually meant for. Maybe that's silly. I feel guilty now that I didn't keep it a secret. To keep it special. Just for us.

"Oh." The man seems surprised. He smiles. "I suppose congratulations are in order. That ring. It seems quite special. Something endearing to your soul."

"Yeah." I feel a bit embarrassed. "It's a ring my mother passed down to me. She got it from my father's mother. Passed down generation after generation. She told me to give it to the woman I loved. Give it to her to let her know that she's mine and I am hers."

"How fun." His face freezes with that creepy grin on his face.

What?

"Just stab me already," I say before I waste any more time. I probably have a stupid grin on my face as well. But mine's the happy kind.

There was a time when I used to drink a lot. My ex-wife used to water down the drinks in secret. She didn't have the courage to tell me straight to stop drinking. I mean, she did at first, but, after a few tries she was either scared or sick of the argument that always started. I was a bitter drunk. I knew she was watering it down, but I never said anything. I guess somewhere in the back of my mind I understood why she was doing it and appreciated it. Eventually, I just stopped drinking. Got sick of the watered down drinks. Didn't want to bring it up to her or go out to a bar or the liquor store.

When it was all said and done, we didn't talk about it. Why I stopped. What she did. Or if I was going to start again. We both knew it was over. The day I threw out the rest of the bottles, I remember sitting on the couch and watching TV. She came up next to me with a blanket and rested her head on my shoulders. We fell asleep like that.

I don't know why I just remembered that.

"Mr. Callahan, you can go," the man tells me. "I assume your waypoint is back to Coldson?"

He stabbed me. The insignia is there.

I nod.

"Yeah, Coldson," I confirm.

Episode 4 👋 Bob And Robert

Why am I thinking of this now?

***

No matter where you've been, the journey back home always feels long. Nasha. Torin. I want to see their faces. Give them a big hug. Have dinner with them.

It's sunset.

If I make it back fast enough, I can do all that with them. If the people here could see how fast I moved through these woods, it'd confirm their fear of the Otherworlders. I always miss these powers when I'm back home.

Home.

This is my home now.

My only home.

What's this sinking feeling?

As if I don't deserve this?

I made the sacrifices. I did what I had to even if it wasn't pretty. Even if it wasn't the way it was supposed to be. I deserve this.

It's okay.

I'll own this.

I make it back to the path.

I see the town, and I immediately feel at peace.

Warm.

That's my home. Coldson.

Serene and peaceful. Basking in the sunset.

I'm tempted to just stay here and let that image burn in my mind. I can almost feel my eyes tearing up.

But no time to waste. I want to be with them as soon as I can.

My heart pounds as I make it down the mountains. It flutters as I think about Nasha and Torin. I can see their faces. Smell them. Feel them. The closer I get to home, the happier I feel. Excited.

I'm in the town and people take notice of the breathless, sweaty, fat man.

You're here, fat man. You made it.

I look up. The smile on my face must be contagious. Everyone who sees me smiles along with me.

Some recognize me and wave hello.

"Mara! Dart!" I yell out their names.

They stop in their tracks.

I run over and give them a big hug.

They're confused. Happily confused.

The goofy Otherworlder.

But I'm so happy to see them. They're my neighbors now. My fellow townsfolk.

Getting through the town becomes a blur of laughter, hugs, and waving. Before I know it, I'm standing in front of my house.

I can't bring myself to open the door.

What if it's all a dream?

All just a cruel joke.

A taste of heaven that I'll wake up from.

The taste I'll forever chase even if I know it isn't real.

The door opens on its own, and my heart jumps a bit.

It's as if my angel sensed my distress. She doesn't seem surprised to see me out here. But she looks worried.

"Nasha," I manage to say.

"Robert." She's tears up and runs to me.

Throws herself onto me.

Allows me to feel that she's real.

That this is real.

My angel gave me just exactly what I needed.

I twirl her around a bit before landing her softly on her feet. We share a passionate kiss.

Some of the townsfolk watch.

We don't care.

I'm sure the look on their face is that even they themselves feel happy watching us.

I open my eyes and everything comes to a focus again.

Two men stop at the mountain path that oversees the town of Coldson.

I'm home.

"Are you ready?" A man wearing a long blue headband asks the freckled young man standing next to him. He's in mostly crimson armor. The breastplate is missing. His hair is getting to the point of being a bit shaggy. But he's given his

nickname One-Eyed because his left eye is always hidden behind a wrap of bandages.

I take Nasha's hand and guide her into our house.

A small army of other men wearing long blue headbands catches up behind them.

Torin sees me and scurries along my way.

"Jake?" The man calls out to the young man again after receiving no response.

"Robert!" I've never heard my name called out so cheerfully… happily before. I can't help but cry as I embrace the boy.

"Yeah," One-Eyed Jake answers. He yawns. At his side is a black helm with long red lashes for a plume. He digs through his pockets for a moment to bring out a crumpled letter.

From my pockets, I dig out the ring.

"Are you…" The man with the long blue headband hesitates for a moment. "…crying?"

I put the boy beside me and take a knee in front of his mother as he watches.

Nasha looks a bit confused, but tears are dripping from her eyes. Happy tears.

"What?" Jake seems a bit confused. His hand holding the crumpled letter ignites with white flame. Some of the men behind him are in awe. Their first time seeing sorcery. The white flame turns to deep, crimson fire and burns the letter to ashes.

Tears drizzle down from the side of One-Eyed Jake's bandaged eye.

"Will you allow me to be your husband and a father to this wonderful boy?" I offer her the ring. She's a bit lost.

Stupid me.

"In my world, we give a ring to the person we want to spend the rest of our lives with. To be theirs forever. This ring belonged to my grandmother and then my mother and now…" I pause for a moment in blissful happiness. "You."

"Oh," One-Eyed Jake finally realizes. "Don't worry. Just a side effect."

"Oh!" Nasha is happily confused and surprised. She chuckles. "I will! Please, let's spend the rest of our lives together!"

I gently grab her hand. My to-be wife is still a bit adorably lost. I slide the ring onto her fourth finger.

"We'll be together forever, my love."

"Yo!" One-Eyed Jake shouts. "Let's start this massacre."

Episode 4   Bob And Robert

Episode 5
IT'S SARNE

"Rape me, rape me my friend. Rape me, rape me again..."

Odd song to be listening to while dropping off someone who hates your guts. Someone who wants to see you dead and piss on your corpse. It's in his eyes. Err. Eye. Jake is glaring at me with such hatred that his one eye is growing bloodshot. I leave him right in the middle of the village down from the farms. I'm guessing this is the village where the farmers sent out their people to reach the magistrate. I see the magistrate's small temple. Their office building. I notice it because I noticed the impostor Redtails watching me from the top of the temple.

One-Eyed Jake should be fine here. Recover. Sober up. Hopefully, go back home.

Before anyone can question the man in the black armor dropping off the man missing an eye, I disappear. I'm guessing the imposter didn't think I would notice, but I chase after him.

Almost immediately, we're already back in the forest leaping through the trees. I forget how powerful this armor makes me feel. I'm superhuman. I'm Superman. A fuckin' ninja Superman. The only traces of us are the clouds of smoke whenever we use the perks of our armor.

The impostor isn't as quick as he thinks he is.

I'm chasing him deep into the woods. Deeper than I'm comfortable with. I'm losing track of where we are. A clearing. There's a temple in the middle of the forest. Seems a bit rundown. I see a statue of a familiar figure. A beautiful maiden with long flowing hair who holds in her hand a book.

This is the temple for the goddess of fleeting moments. Temple of Oslo. I think of her simply as the goddess of time. She and Sarne share a symbiotic sort of relationship. Time and the tales it tells. A scornful wife and an uncaring husband. The top of the temple is an elaborate setup of stained glass where the sun reflects very different kinds of light and art depending on the time of day, and the colors were chosen that each new section to be starkly different. It represents how quickly moments can pass. Good times can abruptly end in a single moment that'll haunt us forever. Or we can just be going for a jog continuing on our mindless lives when a branch falls and stabs us through the head. Or some of us wake up and find out we won lottery. Life's random. Chaotic. And yet most of us are still bound by the feeling that things are fateful. How can it all be random?

Like many other things here, I try not to think too deeply about science of how the stained glass roof works. I'm guessing a dash of Otherworld magic was involved.

But why here? There's nowhere to run.

I take off my helm for a moment to remove the earphones. Wrap it around the player. Put it in my pocket.

With the helm back on, I walk in the temple. There are cracks in the wall, and the wilderness had already started taking over with vegetation and ivy filling in the gaps. Waters dripping all around. There's even water pooled enough to be considered small ponds. But the stained glass roof is doing its job.

Right now, the main hall's ground is an image of a man praying. There are people lined up who don't look too happy to be there. In front of him is a field of thorns with a single tree at the end with a fruit. Above them is a dark, red sun. And a depiction of a wise, handsome, elderly looking man filling up half of the sky watching over them with a worried look. The other half is Oslo who is reading her book.

Standing in the image is the fake-Redtails. He's

CHRONICLES OF THE OTHERWORLD

standing right in between Sarne and Oslo.

He's been waiting for me.

Oh.

I'm one dumbass fish.

Idiot.

"Hello, Redtails." It's a she, and by the tone of her voice it sounded as if she had been anticipating meeting me. "We've been wondering when you'd show up again. We're all curious who you are. Do you enjoy people referring to you by that name?"

Not really.

I'm a bit more surprised at this point that it's a woman.

Which makes me more sexist, that I'm surprised she's a woman, or that I'm assuming she might be hot because of her voice?

Before I could respond, I see a familiar torrent of smoke beside her and all around the main hall of the temple where I stand.

I count seven.

No, nine.

They all quickly materialize into more "Redtails."

Same armor. Varying heights and sizes.

Shit.

Fuck, Sarne.

"So this is the faker, eh?" I hear a snarky sounding guy from the upper levels that looks below at the main hall.

I'm the faker?

"Who do you work for?" The original female I thought was fake Redtails.

I think carefully before answering.

"Sarne," I answer. When in doubt, be honest, said someone who has never been in a situation where saying the truth meant getting their limbs rearranged.

Truth and lies are like anything else in life—to be used with caution and only when necessary.

Fuck.

"Sarne?" One of the other Redtails remarks along with the original female.

"There aren't any royals named Sarne in this Kingdom," a different female Redtails remarks.

A royal?

They think I work for a royal?

"Are you taking us for fools?" She sounds annoyed. "I'll ask one last time. Who do you work for?"

"Sarne." That isn't an answer to her. It's a call.

"Suit yourself." A long smoke appears in the hand of the Original-Other-Redtails, and it quickly materializes as her spear. The golden spear that she killed the Todo brother with just earlier.

"Sarne!" I yell, hoping he'd finally listen because I know he can hear me. He's been hearing me. Watching me. I know it. "SARNE!"

The Original-Other-Redtails leaps into the air, but as she descends, she slowly comes to freeze. The business end of her spear is aimed right at my chest.

There's absolute stillness and silence in the air. I've only experienced this once before.

Sarne.

The entire temple shakes.

Crumbs and pieces of the temple rains above my head.

He enjoys dramatic appearances.

The top of the temple cracks off like someone opening up a crab.

A giant face of a decrepit old man looks in. His burning red eyes are like two suns, and his flesh the new sky. His skin is old, leathery, crinkled, and aged to the point of being bronze. A few long strands of silver hair dangles around like someone taped drapes around his bald head. One side of his face is covered with the countless faces of the lives that once were and that will be like a bad skin condition. Some look simply horrified, some are laughing as if they've lost their minds, a few bicker with one another, and a few are screaming in terror. Children, men, women, and elderly. They're all there.

The most infamous and revered god of this world. The god of tales. Sarne. Or as he and I like to refer him, the god of life. He smiles. Revealing his spotted, yellow teeth. He's missing some in the back. Don't breathe in too much while talking to him, I remind myself. I don't want to puke.

I asked him before why he chooses to look like this and he said it was the most fitting for who and what he was. The form that he felt most comfortable with.

"Tay," He snarls. It's not indicative of whether or not he's upset. This is simply how he speaks. "Tay. Tay. Tay."

His voice echoes through the temple.

"Sarne," I greet him.

"And what brings you back to this world of mine, Tay?"

Gods are very much real in this world. Or at least aberrations that think they're gods. They're possessive as hell like any other gods.

"For a second there, I thought you found a replacement for me." I try not to sound like a jealous ex.

"No, though perhaps if you had more of an appreciation for history and a penchant for learning, you'd not be in the circumstance that you're in now. Like that one girl. Though it didn't do her much good." He cackles. "How much more amusing you and your friends made this world. It's always nice to have more foxes than snakes in a world full of rabbits."

Whoever the girl was that he's talking about, if he found her demise amusing, I feel sorry for her. But I don't really understand his references. The revelations usually come to me later.

"I came to give you an offer," I tell him.

"What could you possibly have that I'd want, Tay of the Otherworld?" He asks as he scratches off the countless faces of lives that once were and lives that will be like zits. The side of his face bleeds with their blood and the mixture of bones and innards. He looks at his dirtied fingers and flicks them off. Then wipes the side of his face and flicks those off as well. New faces… old faces… I'm not sure. Maybe a mix of both poke their heads out through the slime like maggots hatching out of old meat.

"A pure soul from my world. A clean canvas." Perhaps my meetings with him is why I feel so desensitized to violence. I see that disgusting habit of his pretty often.

He looks intrigued. One of the faces on his face is

screaming.

"An unborn child."

"Whose child is it?" He pops the screaming face. Other faces murmur to themselves but quickly grow silent.

"Mine."

"And what do you want in return?" He asks.

We discuss the terms and come to an agreement.

He doesn't laugh nor seem to find our agreement particularly amusing. But he's pondering about it. Even after we agreed.

"Do you ever fear for the consequences?" He asks.

"Of?" I ask in return.

"Of the consequences you'll face once you stop being amusing to me." He cackles. "Go on your way, Tay of the Otherworld. Let's see what kind of tales you'll write and how they'll impregnate others."

Sarne places the top of the temple back again, and all the pieces from the chunks to the tiniest particles of dust reforms itself.

I stand away from the Other-Redtails who'll strike down at the spot I used to stand.

Time flows again.

Her spear pierces through the stone ground and a crack of lightning creates a small crater. I'd have died much like the toad she killed.

She's well trained. Well experienced. My disappearance doesn't faze her a bit, and she quickly swings her spear my way.

"I came to serve Lord Van'Rorik!" I yell as Sarne

instructed me to.

Again. She's well trained. Her spear stops right before tearing through my neck.

"What happened to Sarne?" She asks.

"And Lady Milla Van'Rorik," well, he told me to tell you that.

I manage to get some sort of a reaction out of all the Redtails with that name. Sarne doesn't lie. I should be safe. But it's hard to trust that fucker. I'm nervous.

"To walk by their side even through the deepest of the abyss, as the Abysswalkers," I finish my given script.

"Hey," One of the other Redtails call out to the one holding her spear. "Maybe we should hear him out. I'd at least like to know how he got ahold of that armor."

She retracts her spear.

"Talk," She demands.

I'll play your game for now, Sarne. Follow this rabbit hole down into a fucked up world like a good little Alice. As long as you keep your word, I'll be a good little toy for you to play around with. Your special, voluntary prisoner in the Otherworld.

"I'm not the only one. I'm not the only one. I'm not the only one."

NOT OVER YET...

Thank you for reading.

Now, go leave a review!

It's the best way to help us writers! Let us know your thoughts, your complaints, and, dare I say, even compliments!

This will take maybe 5 minutes out of your time but it'll make the countless hours we spent writing worth it.

Thanks again!

Sincerely,

A. S. Aramiru
www.Aramiru.com
www.twitter.com/ASAramiru
www.facebook.com/ASAramiru
www.patreon.com/ASAramiru

BLACK HALO
the Witch & the Guardian

"With the Light, came Magic, and the Witch. As mysterious as she was fearsome, and as powerful as she was merciless, the Witch almost succeeded in ending the world until she was vanquished by a hero and his comrades.

This is the legend of the Witch and the Guardian.

Centuries after the nigh calamity, this legend is as much as almost anyone knows of what truly happened back then and as much of an explanation anyone has of what ended an era in human civilization.

Though the people may never learn the whole story, you as the reader will follow the days that led up to how a young girl named Lily became immortalized as the Witch though her name, dreams and life became forgotten."

READER'S FAVORITE:
"It is definitely a page turner full of action and adventure."

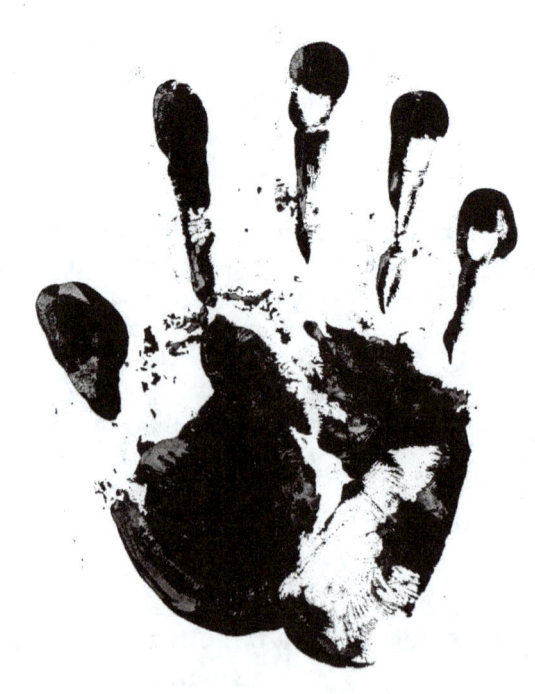

www.ingramcontent.com/pod-product-compliance
Lightning Source LLC
Chambersburg PA
CBHW070324130626
46556CB00007B/2714